DO

CLIQUE

D0735226

Also by Anna Staniszewski

Clique Here

Secondhand Wishes

Once Upon a Cruise

DOUBLE CLIQUE

Anna Staniszewski

SCHOLASTIC INC.
NEW YORK

Copyright © 2021 by Anna Staniszewski

All rights reserved. Published by Scholastic Inc., *Publishers since 1920*. SCHOLASTIC and associated logos are trademarks and/or registered trademarks of Scholastic Inc.

The publisher does not have any control over and does not assume any responsibility for author or third-party websites or their content.

ISBN 978-1-338-68029-4

10 9 8 7 6 5 4 3 2 1   21 22 23 24 25

Printed in the U.S.A.   40
First printing 2021

Book design by Yaffa Jaskoll

Chemistry states the more energy
you put into a bond, the harder
it is to break.
—Unknown

CHAPTER I

Nothing calms me down like science. And since tomorrow is the first day back to school after winter vacation—back to the work-in-progress life waiting for me there—I could definitely use some calming. Luckily, my best friend, Kat, and I are headed to the Boston Youth Science Fair this morning as part of our annual birthday tradition. A jam-packed day of drooling over other kids' projects and meeting real scientists should do the trick!

"I'm glad you and Kat still do these birthday outings, LB," Dad says on the drive over to her house. "What is this, your fourth year?"

"Sixth," I correct him. "We started in second grade, remember?"

Dad laughs. "Oh, right. Slime-making class for you and paint night for Kat. Some things never change."

I laugh too, but really, *so* much has changed lately that I wasn't even sure our birthday trips would happen this year. My parents surprised me with tickets to the science fair for Christmas, and I was so relieved when Kat agreed to come. It felt like a sign that our friendship was finally bouncing back after my ridiculous popularity experiment this past fall. Trying to be part of the "in" crowd, playing pranks on people, and lying to my friends—ugh, what was I thinking? At least that part of my life is 100 percent behind me now.

When we pull into Kat's driveway, she hurries out to the car and hands me a hot-pink gift bag. "Happy birthday, Lily!" she cries. The big day was technically last week, but Kat was visiting her dad over the holidays and just got back last night. It's only been ten days, but I feel like I haven't seen her in forever.

Inside the bag, I find a lime-green headband with alien ears attached. "This is awesome!" I cry, putting it on right away.

"I thought it could be your new fashion statement," Kat says. "Alien scientist chic."

I snort. In the fall, I was all about the science-y wardrobe, which included wearing my safety glasses on my head all the time. I eventually realized that the whole look was a little much for me, but it *was* nice to have my unruly hair out of my face.

"I have something for you too," I say, handing her an envelope.

Kat opens it and frowns as she reads the piece of paper inside. "A ticket to an anime exhibit in March?"

"For your birthday! I figured since you're always talking about this stuff, it'll be perfect for our next outing."

Kat laughs. "I think you're confusing anime and manga. But Hector's always telling me I should check out more anime, so this will be great. Thanks, Lily!"

She sounds like she means it, but I could kick myself for getting it wrong. "How was your New Year's?" I ask, changing the subject.

Kat shrugs as she brushes her neon-streaked black hair out of her eyes. "Pretty good. My dad and my cousins and I did a game night. Then we wrote our New Year's resolutions on pieces of paper and threw them into the fireplace. It was pretty epic."

"What was your resolution? To win even *more* art contests?" I tease.

"That would have been a good one! But no, I decided I wanted this year to be totally drama free. It would be nice for things to be a little boring, you know?"

"Well, without Queen Courtenay around, life should be a lot less dramatic." That's one of the great things about both Kat and me transferring from Hemlock Academy to Lincoln Middle School this year—no more Courtenay Lyons and her minions to torture us.

An odd look passes over Kat's face. Then she nods and says, "What about you? Any resolutions?"

"Not really." I feel silly admitting that one of my big resolutions was about her. Last fall I was so busy pretending to be someone else that it almost ended our friendship. This year, I'm determined to be firmly myself, and to only hang out with people I can really trust—people like Kat.

"What about you finally asking Parker Tanaka out?" Kat whispers. "That's a pretty good resolution."

Ask out my totally adorable neighbor? The thought instantly makes my stomach churn. Besides, this is *not* a topic I want to talk about with my dad in the car. So I quickly shush Kat and start talking about the science fair instead.

When we arrive at the convention center, I'm overwhelmed by the hugeness of the exhibit hall. Somewhere in this mess of people are kids from my school's science club—Priya, Owen, and Bree. Things between the science kids and me have been a little icy since I got kicked out of the club in the fall, but I'm still excited to check out their award-winning projects.

Dad tells us to meet him at the food court at noon, and then he goes off to wander on his own. He might not admit it, but I think he's secretly a science nerd too.

"Should we try to find Exploding Emma's booth first?" Kat asks me.

"Oh, um . . . I don't know."

Kat raises an eyebrow. "I thought you worshipped her."

"I do!" Emma is only sixteen but already a super-famous YouTuber. Her channel is all about using science to make things explode. "But talking to people I don't know isn't exactly my thing, remember?"

"Let's do some exploring first," Kat says, looping her arm through mine. "That'll give you time to prepare."

I sigh with relief. "Good idea."

As we wander down one of the aisles, Kat lets out an impressed whistle. "Wow, this place is huge. You really think we can see everything in two hours?"

"Two hours?" I repeat.

"I figured we'd head home after lunch."

"No way!" I cry. "There are a bunch of panels happening this afternoon, plus the awards ceremony for the winning projects. We have to stick around for those!"

"Oh. It's just . . . I told Hector I'd meet up with him later. But it's no problem. I can push it back." Kat flashes me a smile and takes out her phone to text him.

It isn't a big deal. At least, it shouldn't be. Just because I'm Kat's best friend doesn't mean I'm her *only* friend. I'm glad she's finding her people at Lincoln. Back when we were both at snooty Hemlock, we pretty much only had each other. But that's probably why it's also strange to see Kat with new friends. And doubly strange that she'd make plans with someone else on what's supposed to be *our* day.

Kat puts her phone away and glances around. "Okay, where to next?"

I scan the aisle and spot a brightly colored project up ahead. "How about the physics of roller coasters?"

"Sounds good. Lead the way!" Kat says, and she actually sounds excited. Phew. Our day is back on track.

The morning flies by in a blur of awesomeness. Some of the projects we see are so incredible, I can't believe they were done by kids my age: filtering microplastics from drinking water, tracking aquatic ecosystems, monitoring asthma-inducing allergens. By comparison, all the time I spend cooking up slime and making things explode—not to mention conducting failed popularity experiments—seems like a waste.

After a while I can tell Kat is losing steam. She's trailing behind me, checking her phone more often than she's looking at the exhibits.

Suddenly I spot a tall girl with a headful of tiny braids waving to us from a nearby table. "Look! It's Bree!" I say, dragging Kat over.

"LB, I'm so glad you came by," Bree says to me. "No one's been stopping at my table!"

"It's their loss. This looks great," I assure her. Her presentation on an app that tracks the common cold is a little muted compared to some of the other projects in the hall, but it's obvious how much work she put into it.

Bree grins. "Thanks." She turns to Kat. "It's nice to see you here! But I thought you weren't really into science."

"I'm not," Kat says with a shrug.

At Bree's puzzled look, I explain about our yearly outings. "Our birthdays are only two months apart, so we usually do a science thing for mine and an art thing for Kat's. That way we both get to do something we like."

"That's cute!" Bree says. "So what projects have you seen so far?"

Before I can answer, Kat points over my shoulder. "Lily, look. Exploding Emma is right over there!"

I spin around to find an enormous sign with Emma's face on it a few booths down—and under it, a huge crowd of people obviously waiting to get her autograph.

"We should get in line," Kat adds. "Looks like it might take a while."

My entire body floods with nerves at the thought of meeting Exploding Emma face-to-face, but Kat's right. I turn back to Bree. "See you later?"

"Totally. Have fun!" she says.

As we approach the Exploding Emma booth, my hands are shaking. "M-maybe we should do this later. There might not be as many people."

As always, Kat can see right through me. "Lily, we came all this way! I am not going to let you chicken out." Then she grabs my arm and drags me over to the end of the line. This is one of the many reasons Kat is my best friend. She knows when to push me and when to back off. Without her, I'd probably chicken out of anything scary.

As the line slowly inches forward, Kat glances back at Bree's table. "I don't get why you're still friends with her."

"With Bree?" I ask in surprise. "She's so nice!"

"I guess. But she's still, you know, one of the mean nerds."

"No way. Bree's different." Unlike Priya Joshi and Owen Campbell, the president and vice president of the science club, Bree's never tried to make me feel bad for not being into "real science" or talked me into playing silly pranks on people.

Kat gives me an "if you say so" look but doesn't press. After that we pretty much wait in silence, me trying not to freak out and Kat texting with Hector. I keep wondering if the two of them are officially together, but Kat never seems to want to talk about it.

Finally—finally!—we make it to the front of the line. "Hi there!" Exploding Emma chirps at us, her eyes twinkling behind her trademark purple glasses. "Thanks for waiting! Who should I sign this for?"

I'm so overwhelmed by the sight of her that I can't say a word. I can't believe the person I've spent so many hours watching on my computer is sitting in front of me!

Luckily, Kat steps in and says, "This is Lily. She's your biggest fan."

"Nice to meet you, Lily. Should I sign this for you?"

I manage a little nod.

"She's obsessed with your videos," Kat says. "Last year, she dragged me out in a snowstorm to launch a baking-soda-and-vinegar rocket."

Emma laughs. "That was a fun one, wasn't it, Lily?"

"LB," I whisper.

Emma cocks her head to the side. "What?"

"I go by LB now," I say, my voice growing a little stronger. "'L' for Lily and 'B' for Blake, my middle name." Kat's known me as "Lily" for so long, I guess it's hard for her to switch, but even my parents call me by my new name now.

Emma finishes signing the photo and hands it to me, and I know that's our cue to leave. But something inside me unlocks and I find myself saying, "Do you ever think about doing more with your experiments? You know, stuff that could help people?"

"I *do* help people," Emma says with a laugh. "Explosions are totally therapeutic."

"It's just . . . you have such a big platform. You could get people to pay more attention to the environment and stuff."

Wow, did I really just say that to my idol? But I guess seeing all the amazing science fair projects today got me thinking. If I ever became as big as Exploding Emma, I'd want to *do* something with my popularity.

Emma's smile is gone now. "There's nothing wrong with having fun." She glances past us. "Sorry, I have to keep the line moving."

"Okay. Thanks," I say, hugging the photo to my chest. "I really am a big fan."

She smiles again, but it looks forced this time. I'm not sure she believes me.

As we walk away from the booth, Kat stares at me with her mouth open. "I can't believe you insulted Exploding Emma!"

"I didn't insult her! All I did was . . . offer a suggestion."

Kat shakes her head. "Wow. You keep saying you're back to your old self, but I think hanging out with Priya and Owen really messed you up."

Her words are like a slap. Okay, maybe the old me wouldn't have brought up that stuff with Exploding Emma, but the old me probably would have been too petrified to talk to her in the first place!

Kat lets out a bitter-sounding laugh and adds, "I mean, even your name is . . ."

"Is *what*?" I demand.

"You told me you'd take the best from being Lily and the best from being Blake and dump the rest, but sometimes I don't know *who* you are anymore."

"I—I'm me!"

Kat chews on her lip. "Okay, then promise me you'll stay away from the science club from now on."

"I told you I'm done with all that."

"Just promise me, okay?" Kat sounds so serious, as if she thinks the science club is some toxic cult that's waiting to drag me back in.

"What about Bree?" I ask, suddenly remembering that I can't stay away from the *entire* club. "I have to see her. She's my lab partner!"

"You know what I mean," Kat says.

"Okay. Fine, yes. I promise." I don't know why she's making such a big deal about this, but it's not a promise I'll have trouble keeping anyway. Even if I wanted to rejoin the club, I'm not allowed to. The principal banned me for the rest of the year.

Kat nods, clearly relieved. Then she glances at her phone. "We should go meet your dad."

When we get to the food court, it's already packed. Dad waves us over. "Ready to get some lunch and go check out a few panels?" he asks.

But suddenly my excitement about being at the science fair is gone. "Actually, can we grab some food and head home?"

Dad frowns. "Are you sure, LB?"

I glance over at Kat, who's back on her phone again. "Yeah. I think we're done here."

CHAPTER 2

It's Dad's turn to make dinner tonight, but my sister and I offer to take over. Until a few days ago, Dad's arm was in a cast from a bicycle accident, so he's still a little unsteady with certain tasks. Luckily, he's been sticking to riding a stationary bike at the gym these days.

Cooking with my sister is always an adventure. Maisie never wants to follow the recipe and insists on throwing in random ingredients to make the dish "more interesting." Luckily, I manage to stop her before she ruins the mac and cheese by dumping in a bunch of celery.

As we're sitting down to dinner, Mom rushes in from work.

"Just in time!" Dad says.

"Let me run upstairs and change," she says. "Go ahead and start without me."

Mom got promoted at work a few weeks ago, which I was worried about at first. The last thing I need is more things changing. But even though she's been working some extra hours, it's actually been going better than I expected. Plus, Mom's new job came with a pay raise that helped cover the medical bills from Dad's accident.

As we sit down at the table, Dad and Maisie chat about their days. I can't help thinking again about what happened with Kat at the science fair. When we dropped her off at home, I asked her to save me a seat on the bus in the morning, but she was so busy watching a soccer video from Jayla that I'm not even sure she heard me.

"So, are you girls excited to go back to school tomorrow?" Dad asks.

"Totally!" Maisie says, smiling. Considering she was having a hard time the first few months at her new high school, I'm glad she's back to her usual chipper self.

"How about you, LB?" Dad asks.

"It's kind of strange now that soccer is over and I'm not in the science club anymore," I admit. "I don't really have anything going on after school." Or anyone to hang out with, since Kat is so busy with art stuff and with her other friends.

"That means we can do our homework together!" Maisie says.

Yes, my sister even gets excited about homework. Now that she's "buckled down" at her new school, she's just as into studying for tests as going to parties. After a few ups and downs this fall, it looks like we're back to normal: Maisie has things all figured out—and I don't.

I must have let out a sigh because Dad says, "Are you sure you're okay?" He asked me the same thing in the car after we dropped off Kat, but I insisted I was fine.

This time I can't help blurting out, "It doesn't feel like Kat and I are really connecting lately."

"Ah," Dad says. "I thought things seemed a little off with you two today. But you know, all relationships go through phases. They evolve like everything else."

"But what if a relationship changes so much that it doesn't even work anymore?" I ask.

"It's a risk," he admits.

"Don't worry," Maisie chimes in. "Things will end up the way they're supposed to."

I stab my fork into a broccoli spear. "If only you could adjust for that kind of stuff. You know, factor in different friendship variables and change them based on the situation. Then you could stop things from changing too much."

Dad chuckles. "Like a friendship formula? That *would* be useful. But relationships aren't like that, kiddo."

Maisie giggles too. "They're way too messy to be fixed with science!"

I know they're right. I already made the mistake of trying to use science to figure out popularity. In fact, that ridiculous experiment is partly to blame for Kat and me drifting apart a few months ago—I shouldn't be surprised that we're still having problems. Still, my stomach churns at the thought of her getting even further away.

After dinner, I'm loading up the dishwasher when

I see movement out the kitchen window. I suck in a breath and glance down the street. Sure enough, Parker Tanaka is outside in his driveway, shooting hoops despite the cold.

What Kat said this morning about asking him out must still be stuck in my brain, because I actually consider going over there to see if I can play with him. Parker and I haven't seen much of each other since soccer season ended, but we *are* friends, at least in theory. For a blissful few hours at the homecoming dance, I thought we might even be more than that. But that was before Owen and Priya doused him with ink and I wound up taking the blame. Even though Parker says he's forgiven me, I'm sure he hasn't forgotten. Which means I have no idea where things stand between us now.

What if I went over to play basketball, and he saw me coming and rushed inside to avoid me? I can't handle that sort of rejection, especially not today.

I sigh and focus on the dishes again. I hope Maisie's right and things will end up the way they're supposed to—with Kat and with everyone else.

CHAPTER 3

When I get on the bus the next morning, I spot Kat's neon-streaked hair peeking over one of the seats in the back. She's sitting with a girl who lives on her street. My stomach dips. So much for Kat saving me a seat. I try to wave, but Kat and the girl—Taylor, I think—are talking animatedly about something and don't seem to see me.

I'm about to sit by myself when Ashleigh Webber waves me over. I gratefully slide in next to her.

"Hey, LB," she says. "I love your red headband!"

"Oh, thanks." I adjust it self-consciously, wondering if I should have gone for a more muted color. I'm hoping to get through the rest of the school year without drawing too much attention to myself. Maybe my

New Year's resolution should have been about having a drama-free year too.

Ashleigh, of course, looks effortlessly perfect. I used to think it was because her clothes were fancier than mine, but after getting to know her during soccer, I suspect it's because she's so comfortable in her own skin. Maybe one day I'll figure out how she does it.

Parker hurries onto the bus just before it pulls away and gives us both a wave before sitting in the front. His dark hair hangs in his eyes in the cutest way, and he's wearing the softest-looking sweater. I can feel my cheeks go hot as I wave back at him, a goofy smile on my face. Is it weird that I think even his chronic lateness is adorable?

I glance over at Ashleigh, wondering if she's noticed that she's suddenly sitting next to a puddle of goo, but she's frowning at something on her phone.

"Are you okay?" I ask.

"Fine!" she says, tucking it into her bag. "It's just . . . well, it's a funny story. I have this family friend—one of my dads went to college with her mom—but we drifted apart a few years ago. Anyway, I found out that she's transferring to Lincoln this week. My parents want me to show her around, but it's been so long since we hung out. I'm kind of nervous. I mean, what will we even talk about?"

"You're the friendliest person I know," I tell her. "I'm sure you'll figure it out."

Ashleigh sighs. "Thanks. I hope you're right."

Just then, I hear Kat's deep laugh echoing from the back of the bus. I glance over my shoulder to see her and Taylor giggling hysterically over something. I know it's silly, but my stomach squeezes with jealousy.

"Are you and Kat in a fight or something?" Ashleigh asks in a gentle voice.

"Not exactly. I mean, she's like my sister." I've never said those words out loud before, but I realize they're true. Kat's the one who always understood when my mom was putting too much pressure on me to be like Maisie, and I was the one Kat cried to when her parents were getting divorced. And we kept each other afloat at Hemlock, no matter how horrible Queen Courtenay was to us.

"But . . . ?" Ashleigh says.

22

I shake my head. "Ever since we left Hemlock Academy, things have been so different."

"I'm sure Kat will come around," Ashleigh assures me. "Lincoln must be a huge adjustment. Plus, I bet getting kicked out of Hemlock didn't make things easier for her."

Huh? I turn to look at Ashleigh. "Wait. Are you saying that *Kat* got kicked out of Hemlock?"

"Oh." Ashleigh blinks. "I thought you knew."

"No! What do you mean she got kicked out?"

"I—I'm not sure," Ashleigh says, holding her hands up in surrender. "That's just what I heard. Maybe I'm wrong."

But the thing is, what Ashleigh is saying actually makes a lot more sense than what Kat told me. For years, Kat swore she'd never leave Hemlock, that she'd be there until "the bitter end." It never quite added up that she left simply because Queen Courtenay shredded her art project. Maybe that's because it was only part of the truth.

But if Kat and I are supposed to be like sisters, then why would she keep such a big secret from me?

The rest of the morning goes better than I expected. I catch some kids whispering about me during gym class, gossiping about the silly science club pranks that I took the blame for last fall. But everyone else pretty much ignores me. Phew.

I can't stop thinking about what Ashleigh said on the bus, though. I need to ask Kat about it, but we don't have any classes together. So when the bell rings for lunch, I hurry to her locker.

"Hey, Lily." She frowns. "Why are you all sweaty?"

"Um, from gym class." Not quite the truth, but I don't want her to know that I ran across the school so I could catch her before any of her new friends did. "So listen, I was talking to Ashleigh this morning and she said something about you getting kicked out of Hemlock?"

Kat's eyes widen. "Sh-she did?"

"Yeah. She didn't know the details, but that's what she heard."

I wait for Kat to tell me it's not true, but she doesn't say anything. Streams of kids go past us, but I hardly notice them. I'm watching Kat's face, trying to figure out what's going on behind her pained expression.

"Well?" I prod.

She swallows and looks down at her hot-pink sneakers. "Can we not talk about this right now?" she says finally.

"What? Why not?"

"Because I'm trying to make my life drama free, remember? What's the point of bringing up stuff that doesn't matter anymore?"

"What do you mean? What stuff?"

She sighs. "Okay, fine. It's not a big deal. It's just . . . you know how when we were at Hemlock, I'd go to that brook by the school to sketch sometimes? After you were gone, I started going there during lunch, even though it's technically off school property. I got caught a couple times, and when they caught me a third time, it was my last strike."

"Couldn't your mom do something?" Ms. Edwards is on the board of trustees at Hemlock. I doubt she'd let her daughter get expelled for something silly like that.

25

Kat shakes her head. "The dean basically convinced her that I'd be better off going to a different school. And that was the end of it."

"But why—"

"Please, Lily. It's done. I'm here now. Can we just let it go?"

That can't possibly be the whole story, but I know I've pushed her far enough. Kat is as stubborn as they come. So I simply nod and say, "Yeah, okay."

She starts walking away, but I don't follow her.

"Are you coming to lunch?" she asks.

"You go ahead. I'll be right there."

She shrugs and keeps walking.

My head is swirling. Why would Kat keep all that from me? If it's really not a big deal, why didn't she trust me enough to tell me the whole truth?

Dad said relationships evolve, and maybe he's right. Maybe that's what's going on with Kat and me. But the thing about evolution is that it's happening all the time, to everything. Which means that Kat might have evolved—but I can evolve too. And if I don't, I'll be left behind completely.

There's suddenly a bouncy feeling in my stomach, the one I get when I see an experiment that I have to try. So I pull my notebook out of my bag, flip to a clean page, and scrawl:

Lily Blake Cooper's Friendship Formula.

CHAPTER 4

When I get to the cafeteria, my brain is still churning with my Friendship Formula idea. I wish I could start right away, but a scientist doesn't simply jump into an experiment. They need to gather information first. I'll have to do some serious research tonight and come up with a plan as soon as possible.

At our table, Kat is sitting between Hector and Jayla. At first I'm annoyed that she didn't save me a seat. But then I notice that the chair next to Parker is empty.

Kat flashes me a sly smile. Okay, she's not blowing me off. This is part of her ongoing effort to get me to ask out Parker. Usually he and I sit on opposite sides of the table and don't get to talk much during lunch.

I take a deep breath to steady myself and sit down next to him.

To my relief, his face lights up when he sees me. "What's up, LB?"

"Oh. Not much. You know. Stuff," I answer.

Parker smiles as if what I said was actually a sentence. "What did you bring for lunch?" he asks.

"Turkey." I pull out my sandwich to show him. "Turkey," I say again.

"Oh, cool. I have ham. But I like turkey too."

A long, painful silence follows.

Gah! Why do things have to be so awkward between us? I might have ruined any hope of him liking me like *that*, but I wish we could at least go back to acting like friends.

Just then, Ashleigh appears. "Hey, all! I want to introduce you to Courtenay. She's new."

I glance over her shoulder and almost fall out of my chair when I see the girl standing behind her. I would recognize that pouty mouth and those judging eyes anywhere.

It's Courtenay Lyons, aka Queen Courtenay, aka my nemesis from Hemlock Academy.

No. This can't be happening. It can't be.

Courtenay gives a friendly little wave. "Hi, everyone!"

It's been a few weeks since I last saw her, when our soccer team played against hers. I came *this* close to pranking her in front of everyone as payback for all the horrible stuff she did to me back at Hemlock Academy. But instead I decided I needed to let the past go.

Too bad the past clearly doesn't want to let go of me.

I don't get it. What is Courtenay *doing* here?

Then it hits me. This must be the "family friend" Ashleigh was telling me about. Ahh! What are the odds???

I shoot Kat a panicked look across the table, but for some reason she doesn't seem as stricken as I feel. In fact, she hardly even looks surprised!

"Mind if I sit with you guys?" Courtenay asks.

I want to scream, "NO!" But of course I can't, especially when everyone else is already scooting their chairs over to fit her in. Even Kat moves her lunch bag to make room. So I bite my tongue and focus on opening my yogurt.

When Courtenay's eyes lock on mine, she doesn't glare or sneer like usual. Instead she flashes me a bright smile and says, "Hey, Lily! How's it going? I forgot you go here!"

I don't know what surprises me more, that she's acting like she's glad to see me or that she's calling me by my name instead of "Flat Face" or "Freak Show" or "Super Nerd."

"Wait, you two know each other?" Parker asks, crinkling his forehead.

"Oh yeah," Courtenay says in a sickly sweet voice. "Lily and I go *way back*. Don't we?"

A shudder goes through my entire body, and suddenly I feel like I'm in a horror movie. I should jump up, bolt out the door, and never look back. But I'm still too frozen in shock to do anything.

"And Kat!" Courtenay goes on. "Wow, the whole Hemlock gang's here."

Kat only gives her a tight smile and says, "Hey, Courtenay."

"Oh, right. I forgot you all know each other from Hemlock!" Ashleigh says.

Of course, Ashleigh isn't aware of my whole sordid history with Courtenay. I might have mentioned the evil harpy who forced me to transfer to Lincoln, but I don't think I ever told Ashleigh the harpy's name.

"This is perfect," Courtenay says. "I already have so many friends at this school!"

FRIENDS? Has she completely lost her mind?

None of this makes sense. How could Ashleigh and Courtenay ever hang out together? They couldn't be more different. And Courtenay's father is the assistant dean of Hemlock Academy. Courtenay *rules* that place. Why on earth would she be here at Lincoln Middle School with the peasants?

Ashleigh goes around and introduces everyone. I can practically see Courtenay sizing up each of us. She's probably wondering what Kat and I are doing sitting at a table full of jocks. When Courtenay's gaze locks on Parker's adorable face, I swear there's a little gleam in her eye. Yuck.

"So what's the deal with Lincoln Middle?" Courtenay asks.

Okay, here we go. No doubt, she's trying to figure out the social structure at this school. Once she realizes the science nerds are actually in charge, she'll ditch us in no time.

But instead she adds, "Like, who are the best teachers, and where does everyone hang out after school?"

"Oh, that's easy," Jayla says. "Mr. Owusu, our English teacher, is kind of strict, but he's awesome."

"History's pretty boring," Hector says with a shrug. "But we work in groups most of the time, so it's not bad."

I'm surprised when Kat chimes in too. "Art with Ms. Deen is really good." Seriously, is Kat just going to talk to Courtenay as if she's a normal person and not the demon who made our lives miserable for *years*?

Courtenay nods, taking it all in. Then she turns to Parker and gives him a radiant smile. "And what about you? Where do *you* hang out after school?"

Parker runs his hand through his hair. "Oh, um . . . I usually play baseball in the spring."

"Let me guess. Are you the star player?" Courtenay asks.

Is she actually flirting with him in front of everyone? Last I heard, Courtenay had a boyfriend. Could she be any more disgusting?

"I'm not bad," Parker says, blushing slightly.

"I'll have to come watch a game sometime," Courtenay says.

It's all I can do not to throw up my turkey sandwich.

Finally the lunch bell rings and everyone gets up. I rush to pack my things and dart after Kat before she disappears in the crowd.

"I can't believe this," I hiss. "What is Courtenay doing here?"

"I know," Kat says with a groan. "But I guess it's not a total surprise after all that stuff with her dad."

"What are you talking about?"

Kat stops walking. "You didn't hear? Oh, right. Your family isn't really connected to Hemlock anymore. It was all my mom could talk about before Christmas."

"Why? What happened?" I press.

She glances around and lowers her voice. "Okay, you know how Hemlock was always doing fundraisers for the school?"

I roll my eyes. "Yeah, because one tennis court wasn't enough."

"That's the thing. They never built another tennis court, or expanded the parking lot, or any of that. Assistant Dean Lyons delayed those projects . . . and pocketed the money himself."

My mouth drops open. "Courtenay's dad *stole* from Hemlock? Is he going to jail?"

"No. They worked out some sort of deal. But he had to quit his job and give all the money back."

"Is that why Courtenay is at Lincoln, because her parents can't afford Hemlock anymore?"

"Probably," Kat says. "Plus, without her dad around to get her out of trouble, I doubt she'd last much longer there."

"Wow." I try to wrap my brain around it all. Courtenay has ruled Hemlock for as long as I can remember. It seems impossible that she's not there anymore.

"Of course we'd get stuck with her again," Kat says

with a sigh. "But I am not going to let her get to me this time."

"But I don't understand. Why was she acting like that?"

"Like what?"

I try to think of the right word. "Nice?" But that can't be right. Courtenay Lyons doesn't *do* nice.

Kat shrugs. "Better than how she used to be, I guess."

"But we have to *do* something!" I cry. "We can't let her ruin things for us again." Because that's what Courtenay does, she manipulates and ridicules and destroys. At the end of sixth grade, she yanked my dress down in front of the entire school during a dance, pretty much ensuring that I could never show my face at Hemlock again. I shudder to think what she might do now that she's at Lincoln.

"Don't worry," Kat says. "She'll find some popular kids to hang out with and ditch us in no time. You know how she is."

But that's the problem. I *do* know how Courtenay is. That's why I'm not just worried. I'm terrified.

CHAPTER 5

That evening, I push aside all my fears about Queen Courtenay and focus on developing my Friendship Formula. I've decided to think of it like a chemical formula. If you combine the right atoms in the right sequence, they form a perfectly bonded molecular compound.

If I can figure out the right elements and the right sequence for my friendship with Kat, I'll be in business.

What elements do you need to make a friendship last? I write down.

Well, Kat and I have known each other for years, so I guess I'll start there.

Time.

But then again, it's possible to become friends with someone you've met recently. So as important as time can be, it doesn't seem like one of the main elements. I add a question mark after it and keep going.

Maybe the opposite can happen. If you spend *too* much time with a person, you start to get bored of each other?

Excitement, I write down.

But what does that mean? How do you keep a friendship exciting? Another question mark.

And sometimes too much excitement is a bad thing, like all the stuff that happened when I did my popularity experiment. I wasn't sure Kat would ever trust me again.

Trust.

That's a biggie. How can you be friends with someone you don't trust? But what can I do to win Kat's trust back, more than I've already been doing? Yet another question mark.

I think of Kat's friendship with Hector and Jayla. She only met them a few months ago, but she acts as if she's known them forever. It makes sense, I guess. Hector likes comic books as much she does, and Jayla's interested in joining the art club too, so they have lots to talk about.

I write down: *Common Interests.*

When Kat and I were at Hemlock, our common interest was NOT getting bullied by Queen Courtenay and her minions. Otherwise, we had nothing in common. We don't even like any of the same shows or movies or books or music. We were friends because no one else wanted to be friends with us. But that's not enough anymore.

Common Interests + Excitement + Trust
= Enduring Friendship

Okay, those are the three main elements I need to focus on. Now I have to figure out how to tackle them, one by one.

The whole next day, I'm nervous about running into Courtenay. The only class we have together is chorus, and luckily I'm an alto and she's a soprano, so we're far away from each other. I can hear her too-loud voice soaring over the others' a few times, but mostly I'm able to tune her out.

At lunch, Courtenay is so busy reminiscing with Ashleigh about the "good old days" when they went to summer camp together that I don't have to suffer through her talking to me—or flirting with Parker—again. Phew.

After the last bell, I'm ready to put the Common Interests part of my friendship plan into action.

But as I head across the building after the last bell, I hear voices coming from Miss Turner's classroom. Miss Turner is my science teacher and also the advisor for the science club. In fact, it sounds like there's a club meeting happening right now, but those are usually on Mondays, not Tuesdays. Remembering my promise to Kat, I speed up, fully intending to pass by without stopping.

But then I hear Priya say, "Thanks for coming to this emergency session. The science club's first official meeting of the term isn't scheduled until next week, but Owen and I have an important announcement."

I slow down. Emergency session?

"We feel it's essential to be clear and transparent in matters relating to our club," Priya goes on. "Which is why Owen and I have decided to disclose the nature of our relationship to you."

Huh? I come to a stop and hide out of sight behind the door frame to listen.

Owen clears his throat. "Priya and I went on a date over winter vacation and it was . . ." He laughs softly. "It was platinum. So, we've decided to give the whole girlfriend-boyfriend thing a try." Even though I can't see him, I can hear the smile in his voice.

"But," Priya breaks in, serious as always, "this change in our relationship will in NO WAY affect the science club. We are going to keep things completely professional. The science fair this weekend went well, but we have a lot of work to do on our Carbon Footprint Initiative. We can't let ourselves get distracted."

"Right," Owen says. "We don't want stuff to get awkward. So, yeah . . . Now you know."

There's a long silence as everyone, including me,

processes the information. It seems like this announcement has already made things awkward.

"Well, okay," Miss Turner says. It sounds like she's fighting back a laugh. "Thank you for that update, Priya and Owen. You're absolutely right that we have our work cut out for us with the CFI. Our goal is to decrease the school's carbon footprint by thirty percent in the next two years."

Just then I spot Bree peeking out at me through the doorway. She smiles and waves me toward her, as if she's inviting me to join them.

But of course I can't. I promised Kat I'd stay away. Even if I wasn't technically banned from the club, I doubt I'd truly be welcome after everything that happened anyway. Plus, I have my Friendship Formula to focus on now.

So I only smile and shake my head before I turn away.

As I head to the other end of the building, I can't help giggling to myself about Priya and Owen's announcement. They seem determined to keep things the same, no matter what, but I wonder if that's even possible. If two people realize they like each other as more than friends, that would obviously make the friendship evolve in a whole different way.

For a second, I let my thoughts flash to Parker, but I quickly yank them back. Then I hurry off to my first meeting of the art club.

CHAPTER 6

When I get to the art room, there are already a few kids milling around. I spot Kat and Jayla chatting at a table by the window.

I put on my brightest smile and head over to them. "Hey!"

Kat blinks at me. "Lily? What are you doing here?"

I give her the answer I rehearsed last night: "You tried out the science club, so now it's my turn to try out the art club!"

"Wow, really?" She gives me a long look, and for a moment, I think she's onto me. But then she smiles and says, "That's great!"

"Glad I'm not the only newbie," Jayla adds with a

laugh. "Kat kept going on and on about me joining the club, and she finally wore me down!"

I force myself to laugh too, but I can't help wondering why Kat never tried to talk *me* into joining.

Ms. Deen rings a little bell to get everyone's attention. "I see we have some new members today. Welcome! We'll be working hard the next few weeks to get ready for our open house on February thirteenth."

Everyone around me looks excited at the idea of showing their work, but to me it sounds . . . terrifying. I don't want anyone seeing my pathetic drawing skills. But maybe things between Kat and me will be back to normal by then, and I can bow out of the art club without having to actually take part in the open house.

Ms. Deen sends everyone else off to their tables and focuses her attention on Jayla. "Now, I remember you saying you were interested in pottery. Why don't you go team up with Omar? He can show you how to operate the wheel." She turns to me. "And, LB, I'm trying to think what you've been working on in my class . . ."

She frowns, but it's obvious she doesn't remember. Which makes sense, since I've been doing as little as possible in art class. Normally, I'm a really good student, but art has always scared me. I'm just so bad at it, and I never seem to have any good ideas.

"Well, anyway," Ms. Deen says, clearly giving up, "is there something you'd *like* to do while you're here?"

For my purposes, doing what Kat's doing makes the most sense. "I was thinking maybe a comic book."

"In that case, you and Kat will have a lot to talk about."

I can't help smiling as I go over to Kat's table, where she's already hunched over her sketchbook. My plan is working perfectly so far!

Kat must have overheard my conversation with Ms. Deen, because she looks amused. "*You're* going to work on a comic?"

"Sure, why not? It'll be fun."

"Have you ever even *read* one?" Kat asks.

"Of course I have!" Haven't I? I must have at some point, since Kat is always carrying one—or a dozen—around with her. Right?

Kat shakes her head as if she doesn't believe me. Then she goes back to working on a sketch of a bagel superhero.

I glance around the room and realize everyone else has art supplies but me. I don't even know where I'd find drawing paper, so I grab some lined paper and a pencil out of my bag. Then I wait for inspiration to strike. It doesn't.

The other kids are all wrapped up in their watercolors and collages and acrylics, clearly not struggling to come up with ideas. When I first joined the science club, I was intimidated, but I also had the feeling that I was with my people. Here, I might as well be in a room full of space aliens.

Okay, I can't just sit here. I have to Make Art. The only thing is, I have absolutely no clue how to create a comic. I'll need to do some research on that tonight too. In the meantime, I decide to start with some stick figures. Anyone can draw those, right?

"Oh, is that a bear?" Kat asks a few minutes later, glancing at my stick figure person.

Hmm, maybe not as easy as I thought.

Just then the art room door creaks open and I hear Ms. Deen say, "Hello there. Can I help you?"

I freeze when an oh-so-familiar nasally voice answers, "Yeah, I'm here for the art club?"

No. This can't be happening! Not again. But sure enough, it's Courtenay.

"Welcome!" Ms. Deen tells her. "Let's see. Why don't you go sit at the empty table by the window?"

I watch in horror as Courtenay walks over to the table next to ours and hangs her designer backpack on the back of her chair. Then she gracefully descends into her seat.

"Hey, girls!" Courtenay says.

Kat barely glances over as she says, "I didn't know you were into art."

"Well, I remembered you saying how great the art teacher is," Courtenay replies. "Plus, I've been getting into sketching lately."

I expect Kat to shoot one of her trademark zingers back at her—like "I don't know, Courtenay. You've always been sketchy"—but she doesn't. Instead Kat says, "Cool." Then she goes back to her drawing. I guess she was serious when she said she didn't want any more drama.

"What are you working on?" Courtenay asks me, peering over my shoulder at my pathetic stick figure. "Oh, is that a walrus?"

"Yup!" I manage to say. Then I hunch over my paper and pretend to be completely absorbed in my art, just like Kat.

But Courtenay starts to chatter on and on about how big Lincoln's campus is and how she had *no idea* lockers could be so dirty, and, oh my gosh, did we see her ah-may-zing nail polish? She doesn't seem to notice that neither Kat nor I say a single word back to her.

At the end of the meeting, which feels like a slow-motion nightmare, Courtenay finally stops babbling and holds up her sketchbook to show off what she's done. It's a drawing of a dog, and it's actually pretty good. Way better than anything I could draw.

"Wow," Kat says, finally breaking her silence. "Have you been taking lessons?"

Courtenay shrugs, clearly pleased with herself.

"I've been doing some tutorials online. My therapist says art is good for stress."

Yeah, right. What "stress" is she dealing with? A hangnail? Then I remember what Kat told me about Courtenay's father. Okay, I guess she does have a reason to be stressed. But did she really have to burst into the art club and ruin my plan? How are Kat and I supposed to reconnect with Courtenay around?

When I get home, I find Dad and Maisie eating pizza in front of the TV, which we're usually not allowed to do. That must mean Mom's still at work.

"Pull up a cushion," Dad says, handing me a plate with a slice of mushroom. "How was school?"

I know if I tell my family about Courtenay's return, they'll be sympathetic—but also overly concerned. I'm not sure I can deal with their smothering worry on top of everything else, so I force myself to smile and say, "Good. I joined the art club!"

They both stare at me for a second, clearly stunned by the news.

"Wow, sis," Maisie says finally. "That's great."

Dad nods. "It's nice to see you stretching yourself, kiddo."

Of course, if Courtenay keeps showing up at the meetings, then I don't know how long I'll last. But hopefully Kat is right and, once Courtenay finds snotty friends to hang out with, she'll leave us alone.

As I grab another slice of pizza, the door opens and Mom comes in. "Oh," she says when she sees us eating on the couch.

"Sorry," Maisie says immediately. "We'll move to the kitchen."

Mom sighs. "No, it's fine. You keep eating. I have a few more things to finish up before I'm done for the night."

"We'll save some pizza for you," Maisie tells her.

Mom gives her a grateful nod and then hurries up to the office that she and Dad share when they work from home.

As Dad and Maisie go back to chatting, I chew my food in silence. I'm glad Mom is loving her new job, but I miss having her around.

"Hey, I have an idea," Maisie announces. "How about we do a puzzle after dinner?"

"A puzzle?" I ask. We haven't done one of those as a family in forever.

"I think they're in the Spider Basement," Dad says.

We all shudder. For years we fought a battle with the spiders in the basement, and we finally let them take over. Now we mostly keep the door shut and avoid going down there except to do laundry.

Amazingly, Maisie gets to her feet and declares, "I'll go see what I can find."

"In the *basement*?" I ask. My sister is a total wimp when it comes to creepy-crawly things. I once had to "save" her from a ladybug that was buzzing around in the bathroom.

"How bad can it be?" she says before heading down the hall.

Dad and I look at each other. "Huh," he says. My sentiments exactly.

We listen as the basement door creaks open and Maisie trots down the stairs. Then a long stretch of silence and . . . "Ahhh!"

A second later, Maisie races up the stairs and slams the basement door shut behind her. When she comes into the living room, she's covered in cobwebs but she's grinning. "Got one!" she announces, triumphantly holding up an ancient *Star Wars* puzzle.

"Whoa, good job," Dad says.

Maisie drops the box on the coffee table. "I'll be right back," she says. Then she hurries upstairs to the bathroom. A minute later, we hear the shower turn on.

Wow. I never thought I'd see the day when my sister conquered her fear of spiders. I guess we really are all evolving—and sometimes it's clearly for the better.

CHAPTER 7

At lunch the next day, Kat arrives with a bigger-than-usual armload of graphic novels. My heart sags. Guaranteed she and Hector will spend all of lunch poring over them and ignoring me.

To my surprise, Kat plops down in the empty seat on the other side of me and dumps the books into my lap. "Here you go. I thought these might help you with your art club project."

"Whoa! Thanks, Kat!" I'm not all that excited about having to actually read them, but the fact that Kat went out of her way to bring them for me is definitely a good sign.

Since Kat is looking at me expectantly, I grab one of the books and try to skim through the first page, but my eyes don't know which way to read the panels. Up and down? Left to right? It feels like trying to decipher a chemical equation that's been chopped up and randomly scattered across the page.

Kat is still watching me carefully, so I keep my eyes glued to the page, pretending to be absorbed in it for a while.

"Wow," she finally says, dipping her sandwich in ketchup. "You're spending a lot of time on that first page."

I glance up. "I—I am?" Maybe I'm not supposed to be studying every single picture after all. But how am I supposed to know that? Are there rules to reading comics or something?

Kat and Hector exchange a knowing look, which makes me feel even worse.

"Don't worry, LB," Parker says. "I always get confused reading comics too."

"I'm not confused," I insist. "Just distracted. I'll read it later." Then I slap the book closed and dump it into my bag along with the others. Okay, I need to get things back on track. Time to get back to Common

Interests. "Hey, Kat. Can I have some of your ketchup?"

Kat is obsessed with the stuff. She even carries a bottle of it around in her bag wherever she goes.

Her jaw sags open. "*You* want ketchup? What happened to it being 'the most disgusting substance on earth'?"

"Tastes change, right? I figured it was time I gave it another chance."

Kat laughs. "Sure, help yourself." She hands me the bottle and watches as I put a small glob on my plate. Then I grab one of my fries and dip it in. Before I can chicken out, I shove the fry in my mouth.

Instantly the too-sweet and too-salty taste floods my taste buds. Blech! But I force myself to chew and swallow and smile.

"Mmm, not bad," I say. Then I switch the subject so hopefully Kat won't notice that I'm not eating any more. "I was thinking of doing sets for the play this year. Want to sign up with me?" I was so excited when I saw the flyers around school yesterday. I figure that will give us a new Common Interest and maybe some Excitement too.

"Sets?" Kat asks. She seems to think it over as she chews on a carrot stick. "You know theater isn't really my thing."

"But art is," I point out. "I bet they'd love your help designing and painting the set."

"I'm planning to try out," Jayla chimes in from across the table. "I only had a bit part last year, but it was really fun."

"What show are they doing?" Courtenay asks from across the table, butting in, as usual.

"*The Wizard of Oz*," Jayla says. "It has lots of great parts."

"Maybe I can be one of the flying monkeys," Hector says. He starts making squawking gorilla sounds, and everyone laughs.

"So, what do you think?" I ask, turning back to Kat.

"I guess sets could be a good way to stretch myself," she says. "Sure, why not?"

I grin in triumph.

"Hey, maybe I'll sign up for set design too," Parker says.

I blink. "Y-you want to do sets with m-me? I mean, with us?"

"It could be fun," Parker says, shrugging. "And I've been looking for something to do before baseball season starts."

Oh my goodness. This is perfect. Not only will I have more time to bond with Kat, but I'll also get to see more of Parker. "That sounds great!"

"So I guess I'll see you there," Parker says, and the smile he gives me makes my toes tingle.

For a moment, I let myself imagine Parker and me canoodling backstage. *Yeah, right.* As if that will ever happen. Besides, I need to stay focused on getting things with Kat back on track. I can't afford to get distracted when our friendship is so rocky right now.

But hey, maybe once things with Kat are normal again, I can work on turning my Friendship Formula into a More-Than-Friends Formula.

I'm finishing up my homework after school when the doorbell rings. I open the door to find Ashleigh standing on the porch, her scooter propped up nearby.

"Hey, sorry to just stop by," she says. "I was out riding around and figured I'd see if you were home."

"Come in!" I wave her inside, realizing suddenly how long it's been since I had a friend over. "I was thinking of making some elephant toothpaste. Want to help me?"

Ashleigh laughs. "I have no idea what that is, but sure!"

We gather up all the ingredients and head into the backyard. Luckily, the sun is shining, so it's not too cold out.

"The experiment is sort of like making slime in a bottle," I explain. "You mix everything together and then watch the slime ooze out like someone squeezing a giant tube of toothpaste. Nothing explodes, but it's still really fun."

"Sounds awesome!" Ashleigh says.

We set things up, and Ashleigh turns out to be a great assistant. She watches carefully the whole time and hands me stuff when I need it. She might not be a science nerd like I am, but I can tell she's excited to see how it'll all turn out.

When we're ready, we stand back and watch the "toothpaste" shoot out of the soda bottle. I whoop with excitement and Ashleigh squeals.

"That was so fun!" she says. "Can we do it again?"

"Sure!"

I can't help marveling at how different this is from doing experiments with Kat. I don't feel like I have to rush through it before Kat loses interest, or apologize just in case she's not having a good time. I sometimes get the feeling that Kat is only tolerating my science obsession. But Ashleigh's not like that.

When we're done with the experiment, Ashleigh's phone beeps. "It's Courtenay. She's wondering if I want to go to an indoor trampoline park tonight."

"A trampoline park? I haven't been to one of those in ages." Not since Kat dragged me to one when we were little and I got so dizzy that I almost threw up.

Ashleigh nods. "Yeah, Courtenay's on a big nostalgia kick, so we've been doing all this stuff we loved in like kindergarten. Last night, we even dug up an old dollhouse I have in my basement. Courtenay was obsessed with it when we were little."

"Wow." I can't imagine Courtenay doing anything so . . . *human*. Then again, I can't really imagine how she and Ashleigh were ever friends. But I guess it's possible that Courtenay wasn't always 100 percent evil.

"Yeah, having her around again really brings me back," Ashleigh says, shaking her head. "How are things with you and Kat?"

"Good! Well, better, anyway. We're planning to do sets for the play together. That should give us some more time to actually see each other."

"I'm sure you two will work things out."

I clear my throat. "When you and Courtenay drifted apart, could you tell it was going to happen?" It's something I need to know for my formula: At what point is the friendship bond so weak that it can't hold together anymore? And can you tell when it's ready to break?

Ashleigh fiddles with a button on her sweater and says slowly, "After we stopped hanging out, I think I realized that it had actually been over for a while. It was just hard to see when I was in it, you know?"

I must make a face, because Ashleigh rushes to

add, "But don't worry, that won't happen with you and Kat. It's a completely different situation."

I nod.

But the thing is, it doesn't sound all that different to me.

CHAPTER 8

At the start of science class the next day, I'm setting up the materials we'll need to distill a solution when Bree hurries into the room.

"LB, I need your help," she says.

"Sure. What's up? Did you forget your textbook or something?"

"No, it's about the Carbon Footprint Initiative," she says, glancing around as if she's worried someone might be eavesdropping. "Priya, Owen, and I are supposed to meet with Principal Valenta after school tomorrow and pitch him our top three CFI ideas. But we haven't been able to narrow down the list. Owen thinks we should keep all ten of our ideas and find data that shows how effective they'll be."

"Owen does like his data," I say.

"*Hard data is so platinum,*" Bree says in a perfect imitation of him. We both laugh.

"What does Priya think?"

Bree groans. "Ever since she and Owen got together, Priya's been acting so weird! It's like she's trying not to show any favoritism toward Owen, so she's not saying anything—good or bad—about his ideas."

"Yikes." So much for their relationship not changing things.

"That's why I need your help."

"But I'm not even in the club anymore," I remind her.

"I know, but maybe you could come to the meeting with me tomorrow and try to make them see reason? You're the only person who's ever really stood up to them. They might listen to you."

She sounds so desperate that I'm tempted to say yes. I might not be in the club anymore, but I still believe in the work they've been doing to make the school more environmentally responsible.

But . . . "I'm sorry. I can't."

"Oh. Okay." I can tell Bree's disappointed, but she doesn't push it.

"It's just that I swore to Kat I wouldn't be involved with the club anymore," I explain. "After all the trouble the club caused and everything, I can't really blame her."

Bree nods. "That makes sense. But this wouldn't be helping the club, really. It would be helping the school."

She has a point. If the project works the way it's supposed to, the school's lowered carbon emissions will help everyone.

"This wouldn't be an official meeting of the club or anything, right?" I ask slowly.

Bree's face lights up. "Nope! We're just reviewing our list before we go talk to the principal. Even if you can come read through our ideas, it might help."

I guess if I'm only looking at a list, it won't really be breaking my promise. And isn't the CFI the exact type of thing I was talking about when I told Exploding Emma she should be doing science that makes an impact?

"All right, I'll be there," I say. "But don't mention it to Kat, okay?"

Bree nods with excitement. "She'll never have to know."

On my way to lunch, I hurry past Courtenay's locker. She's squinting at a piece of paper. It's lilac colored and looks like it could be a love letter. Ugh. Who would send her one of those?

Courtenay glances up and our eyes meet. Before I can rush away, she calls, "LB, wait up!" Then she tucks the note into her bag and hurries over to me. "Are you headed to lunch?"

"Um, yeah."

"Cool! I'll come with!"

And suddenly I'm stuck walking to the cafeteria with Courtenay, as if we're the best of friends. I wonder what Thing One and Thing Two—what Kat and I would call Courtenay's top minions at Hemlock— would say if they saw this. They'd probably die from shock.

"You totally made the right call coming to Lincoln," Courtenay says. "Everyone is SO much nicer than at Hemlock."

I choke down a laugh. I have a feeling Hemlock is a whole lot more pleasant now that Courtenay isn't there anymore.

"So have you met any other kids, like from other clubs and stuff?" I ask. *Kids you could go hang out with at lunch instead of me and my friends?* I silently add.

Courtenay shrugs. "A few. I'm so glad I have you and Kat and Ashleigh, though! It makes things SO much easier."

I give her a strained smile. "Yeah. It's . . . great."

She stops walking for a moment and turns to me. "Hey, listen. We're okay, right?"

I blink. "Wh-what do you mean?"

"All that stuff at Hemlock is ancient history, isn't it? You're not like still hung up on it, are you?"

Is she kidding? Just a few weeks ago she was hurling insults at me during the Lincoln-Hemlock soccer game! There's nothing "ancient" about it!

Before I can answer, Courtenay glances over my shoulder. "Oh, there's Ashleigh. Hey, wait up!" she calls. Then she rushes after her.

I stand there stewing with anger. If Courtenay

thinks that was some sort of apology for how horrible she's been and that we can move on and pretend none of it happened, she's even more delusional than I thought. Kat might be willing to let go of the past to avoid drama, but I'm not going to let Courtenay off the hook that easily.

CHAPTER 9

After school, I head past the auditorium, where Mrs. Clark, the eighth grade English teacher, is running auditions for *The Wizard of Oz*. I glance around for Jayla, figuring I can tell her to break a leg, but I don't see her. So I go into the band room for my first day of set design instead.

I hover in the doorway, frozen by the sight of a roomful of strangers. I know Mr. Owusu, my English teacher, but that's it. There's no sign of Parker, which isn't a surprise since he's always running late. But Kat's not there, either. Knowing her, she probably swung by the art room to talk to Ms. Deen and got held up.

Finally I find a seat in the corner, trying to be invisible. A few more painful minutes tick by. I'm considering making a run for it when Parker appears in the doorway.

"You made it!" I cry, unable to hide my excitement.

Parker smiles as he plops down in the seat beside me. "Wouldn't miss it."

"We'll be starting in a minute," Mr. Owusu announces from the front of the room. "I'm sending around a clipboard for you to write down your contact info and any particular design skills you might have."

"Huh, I wonder where Kat is," I say, glancing around.

Parker's forehead crinkles. "I'm pretty sure I saw her going into the auditions with Hector."

"*Kat* is auditioning?" That's not possible. She hates being up on stage. "Are you sure it wasn't someone else?"

Parker laughs. "She was dressed in neon from head to toe. Pretty hard to miss."

That doesn't make sense. Why would Kat be going into the audition after she said she'd do sets with me?

Before I can go try to track her down, Mr. Owusu

starts the meeting and explains how he and Mrs. Clark will be teaming up to run this year's production.

"We don't have much of a budget," he admits, "but I'm sure we can put together something great."

He goes through the plot of the show and the different set pieces we'll need for it, describing the tornado that brings Dorothy to Oz and the big "I'm melting" scene that happens at the end when the Wicked Witch is defeated. "Ideally we'd have a fancy way to make a storm and some fog," he says with a laugh. "But we'll just have to get creative with lighting and sound effects."

That gets my brain going. "Mr. Owusu?" I say, raising my hand. "Um, I could probably make a fog machine. And maybe build something that looks like a tornado too."

"You could *make* them?" he repeats. "How?"

"Well, I saw this video on how to make fog using a hair dryer. You only need to get some glycerin, and when you heat it up, it causes a chemical reaction that . . ." I trail off, realizing that everyone is giving me blank looks. "Anyway, it would look great. And it would hardly cost anything. We'd need household items, mostly."

"I could help build it," Parker chimes in.

"Wow, okay. Great. You two can be our special effects team!" Mr. Owusu says.

When I look over at Parker, he grins at me. "I'm excited we get to work together," he says.

My heart swells so much, it feels like it's pushing against my ribs. "Me too."

CHAPTER 10

Since Mom's been working late a lot, Maisie volunteered to help out more around the house. Which means we've been testing out some of my sister's experimental meals. Tonight, it's pasta with roasted peppers and radishes.

"I didn't know you *could* cook radishes," Dad says, giving the one on his fork a polite nibble.

Maisie giggles. "When I saw them in the fridge, I thought they were more like beets, you know? But you live, you learn, I guess!"

I push mine around the plate, not daring to eat them. They look mushy and unappetizing when they're cooked, and I don't even like *raw* radishes. I scoop up some pasta, figuring that's safe, and am surprised at its crunchy texture. Did she bake it instead of boiling it?

"Do you know what time Mom will be home tonight?" Maisie asks. "I need her help with something."

"Probably not until late," Dad says. "But maybe I can help."

"Okay," Maisie says with a shrug. "It's just that I need a new strapless bra."

Dad's cheeks instantly flare red. "Oh. Um. Huh. Okay."

"I was thinking Mom and I could go shopping this weekend, but if *you* want to take me . . ."

"Sure!" Dad says, recovering some of his composure. "I mean, it's not a big deal. I'm sure I can manage." Then he turns to me. "What about you, kiddo? Do you need any bras?"

A piece of rigatoni falls out of my mouth and lands on my plate. "Nope! I'm all set!" This is NOT something I want to discuss with my father!

"Okay," Dad says. "Well, if you do, let me know, okay? I don't have much experience with this stuff, but I'm perfectly capable of learning."

"Okay," I mumble.

After we finish dinner and tidy up in the kitchen, Maisie grabs the vacuum and a duster. "I think I'm going to work on cleaning the basement."

As if that isn't strange enough, Dad nods and says, "Good idea. Maybe I'll help you." He turns to me. "What about you, LB? Want to give those spiders a run for their money?"

As fun as hanging out in the Spider Basement sounds, I need to figure out the next steps of my Friendship Formula. "Sorry, I have to work on a project."

"Next time!" Dad says. Then he and Maisie happily venture down the cobweb-covered stairs, doing a very bad rendition of "I Will Survive" as they go.

Wow. What was in those radishes?

I head up to my room and find a text from Ashleigh. *I did the elephant toothpaste experiment for my dads. They loved it!*

I laugh and write back, *Nice!*

Can we do it again sometime?

Sure! It looks like I might have gotten her hooked on science. *How was the trampoline park?*

Bouncy! she writes back. *Wait, I'll call you!*

A moment later, my phone buzzes, telling me that Ashleigh wants to video chat. As I answer it, I'm suddenly nervous. Kat is used to me being fidgety and distracted on the phone, but what if Ashleigh thinks I'm weird?

When her smiling face pops up on my screen, though, my nerves melt away.

"Hey!" she says. "So, what have you been up to?"

"Um, eating mushy radishes and NOT talking to my dad about bras," I say. Then I start to tell her about my bizarre dinner experience. By the time I'm done, we're both laughing hysterically.

It hits me how much I've missed this, chatting with someone and not having to worry about every little thing I do or say. I can't wait for things with Kat to feel this comfortable again. But for now, at least I have one friend I can be myself with.

That night, I wait and wait to hear from Kat, but there's no word. Finally I send her a message: *You auditioned for the play???*

She texts me right back. *Crazy, right? Jayla talked me and Hector into it. I doubt I'll get a part, but it was actually fun.*

What about set design?

There's a long pause and then Kat writes back: *I figured it would be a good way to "set" you up with Parker. ;-)*

I can't help groaning at her terrible pun. *Hyuck hyuck.*

So . . . did it work?

Even though I'm annoyed, I can't help smiling as I type: *Sort of. We're working together on a special effects project.*

Oooh! See? It's a good thing I didn't come.

I sigh. I am glad to have the chance to team up with Parker, but the whole point of doing sets was to spend more time with Kat. Otherwise our chemical bond won't re-form.

Hey, do you think you could come over sometime and help me with my art? Those are definitely not words I thought I'd ever write, but I'm desperate. And I really could use some tips. I've been watching some drawing tutorials online, thinking if they worked for Courtenay, they could work for me. So far, no such luck.

Like an art lesson? Kat writes back. *Sounds fun! How about tomorrow after school?*

I gulp. Tomorrow I'm supposed to meet with Bree, Owen, and Priya to go over ideas for the CFI. Not that I can tell Kat about that.

How about this Saturday?

Can't. Have plans with Hector. And Jayla invited me over to watch The Wizard of Oz *movie on Sunday.*

Ugh, of course her weekend is all booked up. It sure seems like with Hector and Jayla around, there's hardly any room for me these days.

Monday? I finally suggest.

Perfect!

And it is perfect. It's exactly what I want. I just wish it didn't feel quite so hard.

CHAPTER 11

Since I've hardly seen Mom the past few days, I try to catch her the next morning before she rushes off to work. I hang out in the bathroom, watching her put on her makeup and blow-dry her hair. It's soothing, actually. I forgot that I used to do this all the time when I was little.

Mom is telling me about the new things she's been doing at work thanks to her promotion. "It's been a bit of a whirlwind trying to learn everything, but I'm loving it!"

"Once you get used to it, you won't have to work as much, right?" I ask.

She sighs. "I know it's been an adjustment. Things will calm down once I'm done with the training, but I'll also have some extra travel coming up."

"Oh," I say, unable to hide the disappointment in my voice.

Mom puts down her hairbrush and gives me a piercing look. "Hon, are you okay?"

"It's just, Dad and Maisie are so good at going with the flow. And I'm . . . not."

To my surprise, Mom laughs. "You and I have never been great at that, have we?"

"What do you mean? You're the one with a new job."

"True," she says, dusting some sort of powder across her forehead. "But they had to offer it to me three times before I took it."

"Really?" I had no idea. Mom's always seemed like such a go-getter. Although now that I think about it, I can't remember the last time she really tried anything new. She's even had the same haircut since before I was born.

Mom nods and zips up her makeup bag. "I've been trying to look at it as a challenge. If I can handle this new job, I can handle anything." She puts a hand on my arm and squeezes gently. "But just think, you started over at a whole new school this year, and you're making new friends and joining new clubs. I think you're better at going with the flow than you realize."

"Maybe. But I'm not sure I'll ever be up for the challenge of going bra shopping with Dad."

Mom laughs and kisses the top of my head. "We all have our limits. If you'd rather I take you, just let me know and I'll put it on my calendar."

"Actually, would you mind bringing me to get a sketchbook and some drawing pencils?"

Mom raises her eyebrows, but she says, "Sure."

Which is good. Because if I'm going to "rise to the challenge" of this whole art club thing, I should get some real supplies.

School drags by. I keep thinking about my meeting with Bree and Priya and Owen, and worrying that Kat will find out about it somehow. But that's silly. Even if she does find out, I'm not breaking my promise to her. Not technically anyway.

After the last bell rings, I hurry off to Miss Turner's room, relieved not to run into anyone I know along the way.

When I get to the classroom, I peer in through the doorway and freeze when I see Priya talking to none other than Queen Courtenay. Seriously, does this girl have some sort of tracking device on me?

"Other kids have tried to join the club because they wanted to be part of our group, you know," Priya is saying. "But you can't fake it with us. You have to really mean it."

I bite back a laugh. It's pretty much exactly what Priya said to me back in September. But wait, is Courtenay trying to join the science club? Maybe she's figured out the popularity stuff at Lincoln after all.

"Look," Courtenay says, "I really want to start off on the right foot at this school. And everyone keeps talking about how great your club is. I'd love to give it a try."

Priya clearly isn't convinced. "We'll let you know."

Courtenay looks so stunned that I almost laugh. I bet this is the first time she's ever faced the possibility of being rejected by someone. "But—" she starts.

"That's the deal," Priya cuts in. "Take it or leave it."

There's a long pause. "Fine," Courtenay says. Then

82

she turns and rushes out of the room, right past me. I try to turn my head so she doesn't see me lurking, but her eyes are down and I don't think she even notices me.

"Hey, Blake!" Priya waves me into the room. "Oh, I mean, LB. Thanks for coming to our meeting. Bree thought we could use another set of eyes. Maybe she's right."

"No problem." I lower my voice. "Hey, you're not going to let Courtenay into the science club, are you?"

"Why, do you know her?"

"Um, yeah. And I'm pretty sure she only wants to join because she's trying to be popular."

Priya gives me a look, and I can practically hear her thinking: *You'd know a little something about that, wouldn't you?* But thankfully she doesn't say it. Instead she says, "I was going to give her a shot, but if you say she's bad news, then I believe you." She unzips her bulging backpack. "Okay, let me show you the CFI list we came up with for the principal."

Just then, Owen comes into the room. I can tell the instant Priya sees him because her entire demeanor changes. Her hands clench into fists and her shoulders are suddenly up by her ears. I've never seen her look so tense.

Meanwhile, Owen timidly inches toward her like he's approaching a wild animal. "Hey," he says softly. "How's it going?"

"Fine," Priya says, her tone even more curt than usual. "We're just waiting for Bree. Feel free to have a seat."

"Um, great," Owen says.

A painful silence fills the room. Wow, I thought these two were supposed to be into each other.

Thankfully, a moment later Bree rushes in through the door and we can get started. We all gather around a desk, and Priya shows me the list of their current top ideas.

"Build a wind turbine? That sounds expensive," I point out.

"Yes, but then the school would be able to generate its own electricity!" Owen says.

I keep reading. "Get rid of all school buses, ban meat from the cafeteria, make everyone at school pay a 'carbon tax.'" These all sound pretty extreme. Do they really think the school will go for any of them?

"So, what do you think?" Priya asks. "Which are your top three?"

"Um."

"Or, if you have other ideas," Bree jumps in. It sounds like she's hoping I *do* have other ideas. I guess she doesn't want to tell Priya and Owen how over-the-top theirs are.

"What if you started a little smaller?" I ask. "You know, plant some trees, convince more kids to bike to school, that kind of thing."

Priya looks at Owen. "What do you think about that?"

"I don't know." Owen shrugs. "What do *you* think?"

"If you tell me what you think, then I'll tell you what I think," Priya says.

They keep going back and forth like that, and I glance at Bree, who rolls her eyes and gives me a conspiratorial smile. She wasn't kidding about them acting weird.

"Hey," I finally cut in, since at this rate, their conversation might go on forever. "How about you give

Principal Valenta the whole list and let him pick?"

"Hm, what do you think?" Owen asks Priya.

"Maybe. What do *you* think?"

And off they go again.

Bree links her arm through mine and leads me to the door. "Oh well. We tried," she whispers. "Thanks anyway, LB."

"No problem. If there's anything else I can do . . ."

Bree nods. "Trust me, we're going to need all the help we can get." Then she laughs and heads back into the room, where Owen and Priya are still at it. Hmm. I guess when it comes to relationships, evolution might not always be a good thing.

CHAPTER 12

I spend the weekend doing homework and researching more ideas for my Friendship Formula . . . and daydreaming about showing up at school on Monday to the amazing news that Queen Courtenay transferred to another school or spontaneously combusted. If only.

I jot all my Friendship Formula updates in a notebook. I used to keep a spreadsheet for this type of information, but after Owen emailed data from my popularity experiment to everyone at school, I'm only keeping a paper copy that I carry with me at all times. I definitely don't want to make the same mistakes I made last time.

"Hey!" Ashleigh says when I slide in next to her on

the bus Monday morning. "How was your weekend?"

"Pretty boring. You?"

"Not bad. Courtenay and I had a Disney musical marathon. I have SO many songs stuck in my head!"

I cover my ears. "Please don't sing any of them! I'm convinced those things are scientifically engineered to get lodged in your brain!"

Ashleigh giggles, and we start chatting about our favorite Disney characters. By the time we get to school, I've only glanced back at Kat and Taylor once, which might be a record.

As I head to my locker, I'm surprised when Kat catches up to me and asks, "Can you check the cast list for the musical with me? I'm seriously freaking out."

"I'd love to!" I cry. Okay, not very subtle. But I can't help it; I'm so excited she's including me. Especially after she didn't even tell me about her audition.

"I was supposed to go with Jayla, but she's running late," Kat explains.

Oh. So I'm the backup. Still, I try to smile and be supportive as Kat chatters on about how nervous she is.

When we get to Mrs. Clark's door, Kat reads through the list and lets out a shriek. "I can't believe it! I'm the Wicked Witch of the West!"

"That's awesome!" I cry. "I'm building a fog machine for when you melt. That means we'll get to work together!"

Kat gives me a high five, then turns back to the list. "Jayla got cast as Dorothy. No surprise there. She was great. And Hector is the Cowardly Lion—that's perfect! And . . . whoa!"

"What is it?" I look at where she's pointing and my mouth falls open. *Glinda the Good Witch: Courtenay Lyons*.

"Wait, Courtenay auditioned?"

"I heard her telling Ashleigh she wants to be 'super involved' this year. I guess that's why she decided to do the play." Kat shakes her head. "I can't believe so many seventh graders got major parts this year!"

"I can't believe Courtenay was cast as the *good* witch!" I say.

"She was actually pretty good in her audition," Kat says with a shrug.

"Well, she does have a lot of practice lying. That's kind of like acting."

Kat snorts. "Exactly." Then she spots Jayla and hurries over to tell her the good news.

As I watch the two of them dance around with excitement, I want to be happy for Kat. But now that she and Jayla and Hector will be spending even more time together, that means I'll get to see her even less.

But I'm not about to give up on Common Interests just yet. We have our art lesson this afternoon, and as we head to our lockers, I ask Kat, "Isn't there a new superhero movie coming out soon?" I can't remember the name of it, but I saw a trailer for it when I was doing some research last night on things Kat might like.

"Yup. Hector and Jayla and I are planning to get tickets for opening night. Why?"

"Think you can get me one too?"

Kat raises an eyebrow. "I thought you hated those kinds of movies. When I made you watch one at my house a few years ago, you spent the whole time complaining that the action scenes didn't follow the laws of physics."

"Well, they didn't," I can't help saying. "But this movie looks . . . fun." Actually, it looks totally confusing. I couldn't understand anything that was happening in the trailer and the special effects looked ridiculous. But if Kat's into this stuff, then I can at least give it another chance, right?

She gives me a "who are you and what have you done with my best friend?" look. But she finally shrugs and says, "Yeah, if you want. But you have to come in costume."

"Oh, really?" I didn't realize going to the movies was like a costume party thing, but sure, I can do that. "Okay. Sounds fun."

Kat looks startled but also impressed. "Wow, Lily. Just when I think I have you figured out, you surprise me."

I smile. "Stick with me," I tell her. "I'm full of surprises."

After school, Kat gets off at my bus stop so we can do our first art lesson. Based on what happened with set design, I was half expecting her to flake out at the last minute, so I'm relieved it's actually happening. When we get up to my room, we put on music and spread out on my bedroom carpet like we used to when we were doing Hemlock homework together. Then we swap sketchbooks so Kat can look at my stuff and I can look at hers.

Her drawings are amazing, of course. Most of the book is full of her food superhero comics, but there are also a few sketches of people and landscapes. There's one of a giant tree standing alone in the middle of a field that really grabs my attention. I may not know much about art, but I can tell Kat's really talented.

Meanwhile, Kat is looking at my brand-new sketchbook and chuckling.

"Um, gee. Thanks," I say. As if my confidence in my artistic ability isn't already at rock bottom.

"No, I'm not laughing at your drawings. I'm laughing at the fact that you barely have anything in here!"

I swallow. "Drawing is hard."

She laughs again. "No kidding. But you learn it by practicing. Not by staring at a blank piece of paper."

"Okay, so . . . what do I do? Because I honestly have no idea."

"What kind of stuff do you like?" She glances at the stack of graphic novels on my nightstand, still untouched since Kat loaned them to me. "Were there any styles in there that stood out to you?"

"Um . . ." I try to remember some of the covers, since I have no idea what's inside. "The one about the, um, lizard? That was pretty cool."

"You mean the dragon?" Kat says.

"Yes, right! The dragon!"

Kat's eyes lock on mine. "Did you read *any* of them?"

There's no point in lying. She'll see right through me. "No," I admit.

"Lily!"

"I've been really busy!" I rush to explain. "And comic books aren't really my thing."

"Then why are you working on one?" Kat says with an incredulous laugh.

"I . . . I guess I just wanted to do what you were doing so that we could, you know, have something in common."

Kat shakes her head. "That's a terrible reason to make art," she says. "What if you focused on a science-inspired project instead? Doesn't Owen photograph endangered species? You could do something like that."

It's not a bad idea. But it feels like something the old me would do. If I'm really evolving and branching out, I need to commit to it. "I think I'll stick with the comic book. You know, challenge myself."

Kat shrugs. "Suit yourself. So . . . maybe it would help if we started with some basic shapes." Then she starts sketching some ovals and circles. A minute later, she manages to turn them into a face. "See?"

I nod. Breaking things down into shapes makes a lot more sense to me. But when I give it a try, the face on my paper is a lopsided disaster.

"Ugh, I'm terrible."

"Lily! It's been a few days. Give it time!" But she must be able to tell how frustrated I am because she adds, "You know what helped me when I was first starting out? Tracing pictures. It gives you a feel for how the shapes work together." She tears the face she drew out of her sketchbook and hands it to me. "Here, try tracing over that and then copying it."

It seems pretty hopeless, but I give it a shot. And I have to admit that it does help. The new face I draw is still a little lopsided, but at least you can tell what it's supposed to be.

"Oh, by the way," Kat says after a few minutes, "I've been thinking about my birthday. What do you think about me having a party this year?"

My pencil slips out of my hand. "Wh-what? I thought we decided no parties."

Kat laughs. "Yeah, when we were seven. Don't you think things have changed a little since then?"

"But you hate parties!"

"I don't *hate* them," Kat says. "It's just . . . I've never really had a lot of friends to invite before, you know?"

That's true, I guess. It's partly why Kat and I started doing our birthday outings in the first place, since at Hemlock we pretty much only had each other. Now that Kat has so many new friends, she could have a killer party.

My throat burns as I imagine celebrating with Kat

and all her friends, feeling even more left out than I already do.

"Are you sure you have enough time to plan it?" I find myself asking.

"I have over a month. That's plenty of time to send out invitations."

"But it's the venue that's the problem. My mom plans events all the time, and she says it's impossible to get a place around here without like six months' notice." It's not exactly a lie. My mom *has* said stuff like that before. But she was talking about big fundraisers, not middle school birthday parties.

"Oh. That's a good point," Kat says, tapping her nose with her pencil. "And if I tried to have it at my house, my mom would totally take over and turn it into a stuffy tea party or something." She shrugs. "Oh well. Maybe I'll just do a small dinner thing instead and plan a big party for next year."

I blow out a long breath. "That's a great idea. And we'll still do our trip to the anime exhibit, right?"

"Yeah, sure," Kat says, going back to her drawing. "If you want to."

Wait. Does that mean she *doesn't* want to?

Clearly my formula isn't working the way I want it to. I've been so focused on Common Interests, but maybe it's time to move to the Excitement part of my plan.

"Hey, I've been thinking we should try something new," I say.

"Like what?" Kat murmurs.

Luckily, I've been working on a list of possible new activities we could try together and have a few ideas ready to go. "How about laser tag? Maisie did it last year and said it was really fun."

"I think that's better with a group of people," Kat points out. "I could see if Hector and Jayla would want to go." She flashes me a sly smile. "Maybe we could ask Parker too?"

Scratch that! The last thing I need is another chance to make a fool out of myself in front of Parker. I think back to the next item on my list. "Or what about a cooking class? There's one starting at the Y soon."

Kat snorts. "Bad idea. Remember that time I burned cereal?"

"Come on, Kat! Don't you think it would be fun for us to branch out together?"

She chews on her lip for a moment. "Well, there is one thing I've been wanting to try, but I don't think you'd be interested."

My ears perk up. "I'm in!"

"Really? You don't even want to know what it is?"

"It can be a surprise."

Kat looks skeptical, and I'm afraid I messed up. After all, normally I hate when other people plan surprises for me. If she flat out asks me what's going on, I'll have to tell her about the Friendship Formula. Somehow I don't think she'll be very happy to discover that I'm using science to try to fix things again.

But finally she nods and says, "Okay, then. Let's meet at my house after school next Monday. And make sure you wear clothes you can move in."

"Why?"

Kat smiles. "It's all part of the surprise."

Uh-oh. What did I just agree to?

CHAPTER 13

I'm surprised to find Owen waiting for me at my locker a couple of days later.

"Hey, Lil' Blake," he says, using his old nickname for me. "Haven't seen you around lately."

I'm not sure what I'm supposed to say to that. I mean, you don't usually see people much after you dump them, right?

"What are you up to?" he goes on.

"Well, I have set design for the play in a few minutes."

His thick eyebrows shoot up. "Really? *You're* involved with the play?"

"I'm trying to evolve." Probably best not to tell him about the art club. He might keel over from shock. "So how's the CFI going?"

Owen blows out a breath. "Principal Valenta lacks vision. He rejected everything on our list. Actually, if you want to come to our next meeting, we could use your help."

"I'm not in the club anymore, remember?"

"This wouldn't be a club meeting. Priya and Bree and I are just hanging out at my house next Wednesday to come up with new ideas we can give the principal."

"Oh, okay."

"So you'll come?"

I swallow. If Kat finds out . . .

But the thing is, I do want to help out with the project. While I don't miss all the drama from last fall, I do miss hanging out with Owen and Priya. They love science in a way Kat—and even Ashleigh—could never understand.

"Text me the info, okay?"

Owen smiles. "Platinum."

I wait for him to leave, but he doesn't. Instead he lowers his voice and adds, "Also, um, I was wondering . . ." He clears his throat, and I notice his cheeks flushing pink. "After you and I were, you know, not hanging out anymore, we had no problem going back to just hanging out, right?"

I blink at him. "What do you mean?"

"It's just," he says slowly, "I don't know if you heard, but Priya and I are kind of together now. Which is great, but . . ."

"But?"

"She wants things to stay totally the same. I think she's afraid that if anything changes, it'll mess up the science club and our friendship and our projects and everything. Like, she won't even hold hands with me because she's afraid it'll make things uncomfortable for other people!"

"Oh." I imagine Priya batting poor Owen's hand away. She's never been a terribly emotional person. I guess I'm not that surprised she'd try to approach relationships from a purely analytic perspective like everything else in her life. But Owen looks upset, so I try to think of something supportive to say. "Have you talked to her about it?"

"I tried, but you know how she is."

I nod. She probably turned the conversation around

so it was all about "the good of the club." I can't help admiring her intensity and drive, but it's also terrifying sometimes.

"She's my best friend. I don't want to mess that up," Owen goes on. He shakes his head. "I really don't know how people go from friends to more than that."

I can't help thinking of Parker and wishing I knew the answer.

But with Priya and Owen, maybe in some ways it's easier since they've been friends for so long. "Well, you already have tons of common interests and spend a lot of time together," I tell him. "And you trust each other, right? And you have fun when you hang out, so the excitement part is taken care of."

Owen frowns. "Are you going through some sort of checklist?"

"Um, kind of. I've just been trying to figure out what makes people compatible, as friends and as more than friends, I guess."

"So what you're saying is that because we're already friends, all that stuff isn't enough?"

"Not necessarily—"

"Like we need to do new stuff together, stuff we haven't done before, so that things *have* to feel different," he says, more to himself than to me.

"I guess you *could* . . ."

Owen nods slowly. "That makes a lot of sense."

"Wait. This is all theoretical, and I'm not sure if—"

But Owen's not listening. "Thanks, Lil' Blake!" he says. Then he heads down the hall, whistling to himself, as if I've just given him the answer to all his problems.

Our set design meeting is in the auditorium so we can take measurements of the stage and sketch out the backdrop. It's also a chance for the special effects people—i.e., Parker and me—to meet with some kids from the cast to explain how our machines will work.

First up is Kat. When we explain the logistics of the fog machine to her, she giggles with glee. "This is going to be so epic!" she says. "I'll have the best death scene in history."

I laugh. "Well, that's if we can get it working right."

Parker nods. "It's going to be tricky to cover the stage with enough fog so it looks like you've disappeared."

Kat shakes her head. "I'm not worried. You guys will rock it." Then she gives me a meaningful look and adds, "*Together.*"

My cheeks instantly get hot. Luckily Parker doesn't seem to notice, but Courtenay—who's lurking nearby—does. Her eyes gleam, and I imagine her filing away this bit of juicy gossip in her evil brain: *LB has a crush on Parker.* Great.

After we meet with Kat, it's time for Parker and me to meet with Jayla to fill her in on our ideas for the tornado.

"We're going to build a huge twister out of foam and chicken wire and hang it from the rafters," I say. "It'll have a strobe light inside, and we'll twist it up so it'll spin around the stage. It'll look awesome when we turn off the stage lights."

"Nice!" Jayla says. "And will I be up on wires or anything? So it looks like the tornado snatched me up?"

Parker and I exchange a look. We hadn't been planning on wires.

"What if . . . ?" I scrunch up my face, trying to think. "What if we rigged up some kind of platform on wheels so that when the tornado comes near you, it'll look like it snatched you away?"

"But really, she'll get pulled off into the wings?" Parker jumps in. "That's a great idea!"

"It might be tough to sync everything up," I say.

"Maybe," Parker says. "But I'm sure if we put our heads together we can figure it out."

Just then, Courtenay saunters over. "Hey, what about my bubble?"

"What bubble?" I ask.

"You know, in the movie? Glinda shows up in a bubble."

Of course Courtenay wants some impossible thing custom made for her. "I don't think we can do that," I tell her.

But Parker is chewing on his lip, looking thoughtful. "Maybe not one big bubble," he says. "But we could probably set up a bubble machine."

Courtenay's face lights up. "That's perfect! Any time I go onstage, I could be surrounded by bubbles!"

"I don't know. We already have a bunch of other things to build," I say. Plus, I don't want to go out of my way to do her any favors.

"But it'll look so cool!" Courtenay insists.

I'm about to tell her "tough luck," but Parker jumps in again. "LB already has her hands full," he says, "but I bet I could put a bubble machine together for you. It shouldn't take too much time."

Courtenay squeals. "That would be awesome!" Then she bounces away.

"That's okay, right?" Parker asks me. "She just seemed so excited."

Ugh. How can I be annoyed when Parker's only being his usual considerate self?

"If you don't mind doing the extra work," I say with a shrug. At least it means I won't have to spend any more time with Courtenay than absolutely necessary.

"Cool. I'll go set up a time to work with Courtenay one-on-one and we'll figure it out," he says.

As he walks over to where Courtenay is flirting with the eighth grader who's playing the Tin Man, it suddenly hits me what I've done. I might have gotten away with spending less time with Courtenay, but that also means Parker will be spending even more time with her—alone.

No. It'll be fine. There's no way Parker will fall for Courtenay's nice act. Right?

I try to shake off my worries as I go over to Mr. Owusu to update him on our progress. But it's hard to concentrate with Jayla and Kat rehearsing a scene nearby. They keep goofing around and laughing hysterically. Jealousy sends a stab through my stomach. If only I'd known Kat was planning to audition for the play, maybe I would have gotten over my intense stage fright and tried out too. But she never even bothered to tell me.

And I still don't know why.

When I'm done meeting with Mr. Owusu, I hurry off the stage so I can't see Kat anymore. I'm going so fast that I crash into someone.

"Sorry!" I cry.

The person lets out a familiar laugh, and I realize it's Ashleigh. "No problem. Are you okay?" she says.

"I'm fine. Are you joining the set crew too?" I ask hopefully.

"Sort of," Ashleigh says. "I'm running lights. Mr. Owusu wanted me to stop by today to go over some ideas for—"

We're interrupted by Courtenay, of course, who can't seem to stay out of everyone else's conversations. Especially mine.

"Oh my goodness, Ash. Do you remember when we were in that horrible play at camp one year?" Courtenay rolls her eyes. "So embarrassing."

Ashleigh laughs a little. "Yeah, totally." She glances up at the lighting booth. "Oops, looks like they're ready for me. See you later."

After Ashleigh's gone, I hurry away from Courtenay and go find Parker. He's sitting out in the hallway, jotting down ideas for a bubble machine in his notebook. As we get back to work, making a list of materials we'll need to buy, it hits me that I'm not freaking out about what to say to Parker anymore. I guess the awkwardness between us is finally fading.

We're halfway through our list when we hear a shriek from the auditorium. I run toward the door and gasp as I see mounds of confetti pouring onto the stage from the rafters, right onto Queen Courtenay's head.

"Get it off me!" she screams, jumping off the stage. Then she starts frantically brushing off the confetti as if she's covered in bugs, not bits of paper.

There's a moment of stunned silence, and then kids start snickering. But I don't laugh. Instead I watch Courtenay's face. Because I know her, and I know any second now she's going to explode. If there's one thing Courtenay can't stand, it's looking foolish.

But . . . the explosion doesn't come.

Instead, when the teacher comes rushing over to make sure she's okay, Courtenay laughs and says, "Oh, yeah. I just got freaked out for a second."

"I'm so sorry," Mr. Owusu says. "That confetti was left over from our last production. It must have gotten loose somehow. Are you sure you're okay?"

"Really, I'm fine," Courtenay says. "No harm done." Then she flashes everyone a smile and heads off to the bathroom. And I realize Kat is right: Courtenay *is* a great actress. But I'm going to find out what's really going on with her.

CHAPTER 14

Monday is Surprise Outing Day with Kat, and I can't decide if I'm excited or terrified about what she has in store. As I walk through the school lobby on my way to the bus, I can't stop imagining all sorts of awful possibilities, ranging from skydiving to mime school.

Then something snaps me out of my daze. Owen and Priya are hanging out on a bench together, holding hands. Whoa! I guess they're starting to figure out this "more than friends" thing. Maybe the advice I accidentally gave Owen actually helped?

As I get closer, I realize that Owen isn't just gazing adoringly at Priya. He's also singing to her. I only catch a few words—something about "we're like two protons attracting"—but it's enough to tell me that it's a love song. Based on the strained smile on Priya's face, it must not be a very good one.

I give Owen a thumbs-up as I go by, trying not to laugh.

When I get on the bus, I'm shocked to find Kat sitting up front, right behind Ashleigh. "Lily, I saved you a seat!" she says.

Suddenly I don't care if Kat *is* dragging me to mime school. It'll be worth it if it means we're acting like best friends again. I feel a little bad about not sitting with Ashleigh, but the three of us wind up chatting about the play the whole ride home. It feels like the perfect combination of old friends and new.

Kat and I go home to grab our bikes and change into "clothes we can move in," and then I follow her into the center of town.

To my relief, we zip past the karate dojo and the ballroom dancing studio. Finally we stop outside a roller-skating rink. "Ta-da!" Kat says.

"We're going roller skating?"

Kat grins. "Not exactly."

We get inside and—whoa. The place is packed

with girls our age. They're all wearing skates and padding and helmets, and they're all skating really fast.

"Wh-what is this?"

"Roller Derby!" Kat cries.

I swallow. Roller Derby? "Isn't that where people crash into each other and get really hurt?"

Kat shrugs. "Sometimes. But don't worry, this is just a practice for beginners. Taylor says it's all easy stuff."

She points to someone on the other side of the rink and I recognize the girl Kat's been sitting with on the bus. I guess this is what they're always talking about.

"So?" Kat goes on. "Ready to give it a try?"

Not really. But I can't admit that. The whole point of coming here was to do something new and exciting, something that could bring us together. So I force myself to smile and say, "Yes!"

We head off to rent skates and gear and get suited up. Then we join the other girls for a warm-up.

The "easy stuff" turns out to be impossible for someone like me, who's only skated twice before and is not exactly coordinated. Kat used to do figure skating when she was little, so she effortlessly glides around while I flail and lurch and wobble.

"Great work, Kat!" the coach calls as we're doing drills. "You're a natural!"

Of course the one activity Kat wanted us to do together has her looking like a professional and me careening like a toddler.

"Keep trying," the coach tells me. But I can tell by the pitying tone in her voice that I'm hopeless.

Kat is clearly having a ball, though, so I try to smile and focus on getting through it. I almost succeed. Then, when we're practicing passing, a girl comes out of nowhere and knocks me off my feet.

I crash to the floor, and for a moment, everything swims around me.

"Lily?" Kat says, appearing over me. "Oh gosh, Lily. Are you okay?"

"F-fine." I choke, managing to sit up. I can't seem to catch my breath, but nothing feels broken.

"Come on." Kat leads me over to a bench and has me drink some water, which seems to help.

The coach skates over to check me out. "Looks like

you got the wind knocked out of you," she says. "Might want to take it easy for the rest of practice. Save something in the tank for next time."

Next time. Ha! As if I ever want to do this again.

I change back into my sneakers and wait for Kat to finish chatting with Taylor and some of the other girls. "See you next week!" she calls to them before heading my way.

Wait. Next week? Is she really planning to come back?

When we get out to our bikes, I expect Kat to announce that she has to go meet Hector or Jayla or whoever—and imply that I'm not invited, as usual. But instead she smiles and asks, "Hey, want to go get some hot cocoa before we head home?"

"Yes!" It's been forever since we did a hot cocoa date at Celia's, a little café near the library. Suddenly I can barely feel my aching muscles. My plan is working!

As we walk our bikes through town, Kat asks, "So how's set design going?"

"Not bad. It's nice to spend so much time with

Parker. But . . ." I shrug. "I wish Courtenay wasn't pulling her whole nice act on him. I mean, doesn't she have a boyfriend?"

I expect Kat to agree with me. But instead she says, "I heard they broke up."

"Really? I didn't know that."

"Yeah," Kat says with a nod. "Plus, her parents are splitting up. Between that and everything with her dad, maybe this new personality is for real. Having your life explode does kind of change you."

I know Kat is right about divorce changing people. Her parents' breakup certainly made Kat a lot more independent and no-nonsense than she used to be. But she's wrong about Courtenay. There's no way she's suddenly changed into a different person. She's as annoying as ever! She's just gotten better at hiding what a beast she is.

As we sit down with our hot cocoas, Kat starts talking about Roller Derby again. Clearly, she's smitten.

"I'm impressed you gave it a try, Lily. I know it's not really your thing."

"It was fun!" I try to sound convincing. I mean, it

wasn't fun for *me*, but Kat seemed to enjoy it. "I'm sure next week will be even better."

Kat coughs in surprise. "Wait, you want to join the team too?"

"Totally!" I cry, but it sounds fake to my own ears. I can tell Kat can hear it too, because her mouth tightens into a straight line.

She peers down into her cup for a moment. "You know you don't have to do it just because I am, right? It's okay if we want to do our own things."

"Yeah, I know. But isn't it nice to do something together?"

"Of course it is. But no offense, Lil. I don't think Roller Derby is for you."

I can't argue with that. Because she's right. I pretty much hated every minute of it.

"You're still coming to the movie this weekend, right?" she adds.

I swallow a too-hot sip of cocoa and nod. Roller Derby might have been a bust, but I know I can get my plan back on track. "Wouldn't miss it for anything," I say.

CHAPTER 15

When it's time for another art club meeting, I'm surprised to realize that I'm not dreading it this time. While my art is still pathetic and I have to suffer through seeing Courtenay yet again, things with Kat feel so much better now. And our Roller Derby outing even gave me a great idea for a comic book.

"Look what I came up with last night!" I tell Kat. I pull out my sketchbook and show her some ideas I had for a superhero I'm calling Uncoordinated Girl. "Her superpower is that she's always falling over and messing stuff up, but that ends up helping her accidentally save the day."

Kat chuckles. "That's awesome, Lily. And I like

how you're keeping the art really simple and kid-like. It's an interesting stylistic choice."

I nod, pretending like I *meant* for my pathetic stick figures to look like something a little kid would draw. All that matters is that Kat seems impressed with what I'm doing. And oddly, I'm actually excited to keep working on the project. Every time I think about it, more ideas pop into my head.

When I glance around, I notice that Courtenay's not here yet. Maybe she finally found some other people to torment and she quit the club. This day just keeps getting better!

But a few minutes later, the art room door opens and Courtenay comes in. For some reason, her hair is sopping wet.

"Did you join the swim team or something?" I ask.

Courtenay shakes her head. "No. I got gum in my hair. Had to go wash it out in the bathroom."

"Yuck," Jayla says with a sympathetic smile. "How did that happen?"

"There was some stuck to my backpack and I didn't notice until it got on me," Courtenay says. "Someone must have put it there by accident." Then, for some reason, she gives me a piercing look and asks, "Right, LB?"

I blink, suddenly flustered. "R-right."

Courtenay nods, as if that's the correct response. Then she grabs her sketchbook and starts drawing. And as if that isn't strange enough, for the rest of the meeting, she doesn't say another word.

The next day, I head to Owen's house for another CFI brainstorming session. I haven't been there since last summer, when I tagged along with Maisie to a pool party hosted by Owen's older brother, Wyatt. That was back when I was just starting my popularity experiment and Kat was still firmly my best friend. It seems like a lifetime has gone by since then.

Owen's mom waves me inside and sends me up to Owen's room. Climbing the stairs, I hear laughter echoing down the hall. I knock on the door and peek in.

Inside, Owen and Priya are sitting very close together on the bed while Bree is on the floor with a grimace on her face.

"Hey!" Owen says when he sees me. "Come on in. I was just telling Bree and Pumpkin about some new recycling ideas."

I blink. "Pumpkin?"

"He means me," Priya says flatly.

Owen chuckles. "Oh, sorry. Sometimes I don't even notice I'm saying it."

"Yeah," Bree says. "He uses it *a lot*." Maybe that's why she looks like she's in pain.

"Pull up a chair," Owen tells me.

I sit down at Owen's desk and listen as he explains his plan for an even more complicated recycling system than the school has already. "What do you think, Lil' Blake?"

"Well . . . to be honest . . . I think the system we have is already pretty confusing. Do we really want to add more options?"

Owen rolls his eyes. "I think people can deal with a little confusion if it means saving the planet, don't you?"

"Totally! But we don't want them to get frustrated."

"Then even more stuff will get thrown out," Bree adds.

Owen groans. "I guess that's true." He turns to Priya and puts his arm around her shoulders. "Pumpkin, did you have any ideas?"

"I came up with a few," Priya says, wriggling free from Owen to get her laptop. She starts listing off ideas that are even more ridiculous than the ones on the original list. When she's done, we all stare at her for a moment.

"I'm sorry. Did you say the school should rent *goats* to mow the athletic fields?" Bree asks slowly.

"That way we don't feed any gas-guzzling lawn mowers!" Priya says.

"True," Bree says. "But we do have to feed the goats, which could get expensive." She looks to me for help.

"Also, goats poop, right?" I jump in. "So wouldn't there be goat poop all over the soccer field and stuff?" I don't exactly want to deal with that during a game.

Priya blinks. "Oh. You're right. Forget it."

"No!" Owen cries. "I think it's a great idea! The

school could collect the goat poop and use it as fertilizer!"

"You really think the principal will go for that?" Bree asks, crinkling her nose.

"Of course! It's brilliant." He turns to Priya. "*You're* brilliant."

Priya gives him a shy smile and says, "You're the one who came up with the fertilizer part. It's genius."

Owen blushes. "Thanks."

After that, the meeting goes completely off the rails. Bree and I sit there listening as Priya and Owen cheer on each other's increasingly bizarre ideas. No doubt Principal Valenta will laugh in their faces if they suggest any of them.

I'm actually relieved when it's time to head home.

"Who knew Priya and Owen agreeing on everything would make things worse?" Bree whispers to me as we leave the house.

"I know," I whisper back. "I almost miss the good old days when they were too afraid to have an opinion!"

CHAPTER 16

On Saturday morning, Parker and I have a plan to get together again to work on special effects. We've sketched out our tornado and tracked down the materials, but now we have to figure out how to make the whole thing structurally sound and attach it to a moving platform for Jayla. We've decided to split up the other projects to make things easier, so Parker will keep working on the bubble maker and I'll build the fog machine on my own. If we keep going at this rate, we'll be in good shape.

Even though Parker lives a few doors down from us, I've never been inside his house before. I'm shaking with nerves as I put on my favorite jeans and a dark-colored T-shirt that I hope will conceal any sweat stains. Perspiration is a typical human stress reaction, but when I'm around Parker, my sweat glands seem to go into overdrive.

When I've tamed my unruly hair as much as possible, I take a deep breath and head over. My brain is telling me to flee the whole way over, but since Parker's house is so close, before I know it, I'm standing on his front porch and it's too late to back out.

"LB!" he says when he opens the door. "Come in. There's something I want to show you."

He waves for me to follow him, and we go down into the finished basement. There's a big TV set up on one wall and some comfy-looking couches. But what grabs my attention is a large table in the corner. It's holding up the biggest Lego structure I've ever seen.

"Whoa," I say, heading straight for it. "The International Space Station!" It doesn't look quite finished yet, but I'd recognize that design anywhere.

"They have ISS Lego kits," Parker says, coming up beside me. "But we decided to make our own. Totally nerdy, right?"

"No, it's incredible. This must have taken forever."

He smiles. "My mom and I have been working on it since I was little. Every once in a while, we'll put on a new section."

"That's awesome. I love that you and your mom build stuff together." My mom's become more open-minded about my "science-y stuff," but I can't imagine her ever doing any of it with me.

"We're both really into space exploration." He shrugs. "I know it's a long shot, but I'd love to help build real spaceships one day."

Oh my goodness. I didn't think it was possible for me to like Parker even more than I already do!

"Here's what I wanted to show you." Parker grabs a box from under the table and hands it to me. "I found a used set online and had to get it."

As I hold the box, staring at the picture on the side, it takes me a second to understand what I'm looking at. Then I can't help laughing in disbelief.

"Is that a Lego *chemistry lab*?" I practically shriek.

"Yes!" Parker says. "I figured it perfectly combines our interests, right? I love Legos and you love chemistry."

"That's amazing!"

"So what do you think? Should we start building it? I know we have to work on our special effects stuff too, so we probably won't get very far, but you can come back anytime so we can finish it."

Oh my goodness. He wants me to COME BACK. He wants us to BUILD IT TOGETHER. He bought it BECAUSE OF ME! There are not enough all-caps to express how ridiculously excited I am!

I hand the box back to him, and as Parker reaches out to take it, our fingers touch. He looks at me with a shy smile.

Kapow! A bolt of electricity seems to zap through me. Is it possible . . . Is he thinking about . . . KISSING ME???

My brain floods with images: all those times I spied on him out my kitchen window, all those times Kat made fun of me for denying that I liked him, and the amazing feeling of seeing Parker at the homecoming dance waiting for me with an origami flower. And then that horrible moment when he was doused with ink because of my silly fight with Owen, and that day I showed up at his front door and he refused to even talk to me because he was so betrayed. I can't believe that after all that, Parker wants to kiss me! I'm just sorry I put him through it in the first place.

"I'm sorry," I whisper as Parker's lips inch toward mine.

Parker freezes. "What?"

"No, I—I didn't mean—" I stammer, but before I can explain, the basement door creaks open.

"Parker?" his mom calls down the stairs.

Parker and I jump apart as if we've been caught doing something. (*Were* we doing something? Was he really about to kiss me? And did I really ruin it by apologizing???)

"Yeah?" Parker calls back, looking as flustered as I feel.

I take a deep breath and close my eyes, trying to pull myself together.

"Your friend Courtenay is calling," his mom says. "She said you weren't answering her texts, so she tried the house phone instead."

Parker blinks. I expect him to tell his mom that

he'll call Courtenay back later. (I mean, why is she even calling him in the first place?) But he clears his throat and calls up, "Be right there!" Then he gives me an uncertain smile. "This'll only take a minute, okay?"

"Sure. I'll, uh, start working on stuff."

He nods and hurries upstairs. As I watch him disappear, my heart is still pounding. What just happened?

CHAPTER 17

When I get to the mall that night, I'm already sweating in the cow costume that Dad helped me pick out. I don't know how I'm going to sit through a whole movie in this thing. But Kat would kill me if I didn't show up in costume, so I decided to go big. I can't wait to tell Kat about my almost kiss with Parker. She is going to freak out!

It takes me a while to find Kat, Jayla, and Hector because they're dressed up in costumes that look a lot like what everyone else is wearing.

"There you are!" I finally say when I spot Kat's neon-streaked hair peeking out from under an elaborate headpiece. "This place is nuts!"

She jumps at the sight of me. "Lily? Is that you in there?"

Hector laughs. "What kind of costume is that?"

I swallow. "Um . . ." Because that's when it hits me—no one else is dressed like they're at a costume party. They're all dressed like the characters from the movie. I don't know any of the characters' names, but I vaguely remember them from the movie trailer.

Suddenly, Courtenay steps forward, all decked out in a costume and makeup that look like they were done by a professional. Ugh, of course she's here. I don't even know why I'm surprised to see her anymore.

"Oh," Courtenay says to me, "are you one of the Oriflax?" When I stare at her blankly, she adds, "You know, the aliens that they fight in the movie? They're big and spotted, right?"

Wait. Is she actually trying to help me? Or is this some sort of trap? I'm so desperate to save face that I risk going with it.

"Yup! I was going for Oriflax, but this was the best I could do."

To my relief, Hector says, "Good thinking!" He laughs again, but this time it's a much nicer sound.

I can see Kat frowning at me, though, and it's

obvious she knows I'm full of it. But how was I supposed to know what she meant by "wear a costume"?

Although . . . now that I'm thinking about it, I do remember Kat showing me pictures of when she and her dad went to a movie on opening night last year, all dressed up as aliens. So, okay, fine, maybe I had *some* idea.

"Let's go in," Kat says, passing out the tickets.

"What is Courtenay doing here?" I hiss as she hands me mine.

Kat shrugs. "She invited herself along. What was I supposed to do?"

"Tell her *no*?"

"Come on, Lily," she says. "No more drama, remember?" Which is a funny thing to say after she's invited the biggest drama queen on earth to hang out with us.

When the movie starts, it's loud and overwhelming and I can hardly follow half the plot, but I'm surprised to find myself actually enjoying it by the end. I still can't remember any characters' names, but some of the action scenes are pretty fun to watch. And they get the physics down a lot better in the actual movie than in the trailer.

At one point, I even laugh along with the rest of the audience. I glance over at Kat and see her looking back at me, smiling.

After the movie, I'm chatting and laughing with the others. Shockingly, it turns out Courtenay is a superfan and knows all the details. Unless she's only pretending like I am—but if she is, I have to admit she's really good at it.

Even with Courtenay there, it's so great to be part of a group again. I haven't felt this way since I was in the science club, and this time is even better because Kat is part of it too. All the weirdness of the past few weeks seems to have melted away.

Now that I'm actually talking to Hector, I can understand why Kat likes him so much. He's hilarious. The way he reenacts some of the scenes from the movie has us all in hysterics.

"I have an idea," Jayla announces. "We should go bowling in our costumes!"

We all cheer in response. Bowling isn't exactly my

forte—that pesky coordination again—but it's bound to be less traumatizing than Roller Derby.

"I want to grab some candy before we go," Courtenay says. "Meet you there?"

"Sounds good!" Jayla says.

As we head to the bowling place, I'm pleasantly surprised when Kat comes over and puts her arm around my bovine-printed shoulders. "I'm so glad you came."

"Moooo too," I say.

She snorts at my silly joke. Then her smile fades slightly. "I'm sorry. I should have told you Courtenay was coming. I know you don't love having her around. But maybe it's time you gave her a chance."

I nod, but I'm not even really thinking about Courtenay. I'm thinking about Kat and how it finally feels like I have my best friend back.

"Hey, I could use your advice," I whisper. Then I fill her in on what happened in Parker's basement.

"So he almost kissed you and then you apologized and he ran away?" she asks, her eyes wide.

"Yes! Is that bad? Do you think he hates me now?"

After he came back down from talking to Courtenay, we worked on the tornado for a while, but we hardly said a word to each other.

"He's probably confused," Kat says. "Next time you see him, just explain what happened. He'll understand."

Right. Explain what happened. I can do that without dying from embarrassment. Maybe.

"Lily, are you okay? You look like you might pass out."

"It's my costume. It's really hot," I say, and it's the truth—though thinking about Parker obviously isn't helping, either. "I'll go take it off and meet you at the bowling alley, okay?"

I head off toward the bathroom, hoping the shirt I'm wearing underneath isn't soaked through with sweat.

Suddenly I spot Courtenay at the concession stand. But she's not alone. Thing One and Thing Two—her BFFs from Hemlock—are there too. Their names are actually Brinley and Savannah, but in all the years I knew them they never actually spoke to me, so I refuse to think about them as anything other than Courtenay's minions.

I hear one of the Things let out a cackling laugh, and my stomach turns cold. Are they laughing about us? Maybe that's been Courtenay's scheme all along: hang out with Kat and me, and then report back to her minions as if we're a big joke.

I try to approach unnoticed, which is not easy when you're dressed as a cow. But I'm able to tuck myself behind a nearby sign and eavesdrop.

"You're here with a bunch of losers?" Thing One is saying. "I know your new school is lame, but Kat Edwards and Lily Cooper, really?"

Thing Two titters. "I can't believe they'd even give you the time of day after all the stuff you did to them. I mean, that whole dress thing at the dance last year? Hilarious!"

"And getting Kat kicked out of Hemlock," Thing One adds. "Does she even know it was you?"

Courtenay glances around. "Shh, keep your voice down."

"What, are you afraid they'll find out what you're really like?" Thing One asks.

Thing Two snorts. "Too late for that!"

Then they both burst out laughing. I don't wait around to hear Courtenay join in.

Instead I stumble away, my blood pounding in my ears as I try to make sense of what I heard. Courtenay got Kat kicked out of Hemlock? How?

Oh . . . she must have been the one to turn Kat in for leaving school grounds! She's the reason Kat had to leave Hemlock and come to Lincoln. And now she and her minions are standing around laughing about it.

I knew it. I *knew* Courtenay hadn't changed. I knew her niceness was an act. And finally I have proof.

"Kat, I have to talk to you," I say when I find her in the bowling alley. I need to get this out before Courtenay shows up. No doubt she'll deny everything. "It's about Courtenay."

Kat rolls her eyes. "Lily . . ."

"No, listen to me. I just heard her talking to the Things. They were at the movie theater! Courtenay's the one who got you kicked out of Hemlock. She's the one who turned you in!"

"Lily, stop."

"I get that you think she's changed, but she hasn't! She's the same old Courtenay and this is all a joke to her and—"

"Lily!" Kat cries. "I know, okay? I know she was the one who got me in trouble. She told me the first week she was at Lincoln."

I blink. "Wh-what?"

"Courtenay apologized. It was a mistake and she regrets it and it's over."

"But it's not over! You should have heard her with her friends just now, Kat. They were laughing at us. I'm telling you, you can't trust Courtenay. She's evil!"

Suddenly Kat's eyes snap up and I can tell by the guilty expression on her face that Courtenay is right behind me.

As she comes up beside me, I expect her to deny everything or to make up some bizarre explanation for what I heard. But instead, Courtenay surprises me by saying, "So you really are the one who's been playing those pranks on me."

I blink. "What pranks?"

"The mean notes in my locker. The gum. The

confetti. I heard rumors you did that kind of stuff to people, but I didn't think you hated me enough to do it to *me*."

Kat's mouth falls open. "Lily, is that true?"

"No! I didn't even know about the notes. And the confetti was an accident. Even Mr. Owusu said so."

"Pretty convenient accident," Courtenay says softly.

Kat still looks incredulous. "Is this another science club thing? Are you pulling pranks with them again?"

"I told you. I'm done with the science club!" I cry.

Courtenay starts to say something, but then falls silent. I whirl to face her. "What?" I demand. "If you have something to say, just say it!"

Courtenay shakes her head. "It's just . . . I saw you going into that meeting with Priya."

Kat's eyes narrow. "What meeting?"

Uh-oh. "It was nothing! I helped out with some stuff for the Carbon Footprint Initiative, that's all. Bree asked for my input, so I met with Priya and Owen to—"

"So you *have* been hanging out with them," Kat says. "Even though you promised you wouldn't anymore."

I shake my head. "You know how important science is to me. I can't completely cut it out of my life. It's not that simple."

"But it *is* that simple," Kat says flatly.

"Kat, please. Just trust me—"

"Trust you? Are you serious?" She lets out an odd laugh. "When I first got to Lincoln, you weren't even Lily anymore. You were some stranger named Blake. You kept lying and pulling pranks and trying to make me into someone I'm not. Yes, you apologized. Yes, I forgave you. But I can't start trusting you again overnight, *especially* not when you're lying to me again!"

I open my mouth to argue, but I don't know what to say.

"Just give me some time, okay?" Kat adds. Then she turns and walks away.

CHAPTER 18

I spend most of Sunday morning in bed, moping. Ashleigh sends me some cute puppy videos, which I guess means she heard about my fight with Kat. I appreciate that she's trying to cheer me up, and that she didn't automatically take Courtenay's side. But even the sight of a litter of puppies in tiny bow ties can't snap me out of my funk.

When I finally drag myself out of bed, I stare at my Friendship Formula for a while, tempted to tear it out of my notebook and rip it to shreds. But the thing that stops me is the knowledge that my formula *was* working!

Common Interests + Excitement + Trust
= Enduring Friendship

For a while, anyway, Kat and I really were reconnecting. And it wasn't simply because we were spending more time together. We were joking around and confiding in each other. Yes, there were still bumps in the road, but we were on our way! She was finally starting to trust me again! And then Courtenay showed up and ruined it, like she ruins everything.

Well, if Kat wants time apart, I can give her that. Maybe it will make her realize how much she misses not having me around.

The thing is, I can't remember the last time I was completely on my own. Even when I was at Lincoln and Kat was still at Hemlock, I could count on her for advice and moral support.

I think back to my New Year's resolution about being totally myself. Do I even know who that is? For so long, I was Kat's sidekick or Maisie's little sister. When I joined the science club, I became whoever Priya and Owen wanted me to be.

Maybe this time away from Kat isn't the worst thing. Maybe it's finally a chance to figure out who I am. And to prove to Kat how fine I can be without her.

When I see Kat on the bus on Monday morning, she gives me a little nod and then looks away. At least she didn't completely ignore me. I guess that's something.

When I slide in next to Ashleigh, I'm relieved when she whispers, "I know you wouldn't do that stuff Courtenay accused you of."

"Thanks," I whisper back. "After everything that happened this fall, I guess I can't blame people for thinking it was me. And if anyone has good reason to prank Courtenay, it's me."

Ashleigh frowns. "What do you mean?"

But that's not something I want to get into right now, especially with Ashleigh, so I say, "We didn't really get along at Hemlock, that's all."

"Oh. Well, you don't seem like someone who'd hold a grudge," Ashleigh says.

I shrug. I'm not sure that's true, but if I could get Courtenay out of my life, I'd happily never think about her again.

I'm nervous about seeing Parker after our almost

kiss. I know I need to talk to him like Kat said, but he's so late getting on the bus that he slides into his seat without even glancing in my direction. And when we get to school, he hurries inside without so much as a wave. Maybe he has a meeting with a teacher or something.

At lunch, I can't deal with the stress of seeing Kat, so I head to the library to work on my special effects project. My fog machine, at least, is going great. I had Dad bring me to the hardware store last night to get materials. Now I need to take the hair dryer apart, make some modifications, and then build a new case around it. The best part is that I'll be able to hold the machine in my hands and spray the fog where it needs to go. That will make it easier for Kat to sneak off the stage and make it look like she disappeared.

I'm excited to tell Parker about my progress at set design that afternoon. Now that the show is only a month away, Mr. Owusu has scheduled some extra sessions in the band room after school.

But when I get there, there's no sign of Parker. After a few minutes, everyone else trickles in, but

Parker still isn't there. I think back to how he practically ran off the bus this morning. Is it possible he's avoiding me?

Okay, maybe I'm jumping to conclusions. Maybe there's another explanation. (Please let there be another explanation.)

I go over to Mr. Owusu and ask, "Do you know if Parker Tanaka is coming today?"

He glances up from his clipboard. "Parker? He asked if he could spend today's session in the woodshop working on the structural elements for the tornado."

"Oh." I thought we were supposed to work on that together. Why would he go down there without me? "Can I go too?"

"Sure," he says. "But try to use the time to work, not to socialize, okay?"

I blush, wondering if he's seen us talking—flirting?—in the past.

When I get to the woodshop, I find Parker at a back table cutting pieces of foam. I hover near a shelf of safety glasses, trying to work up the courage to go talk to him. I'm so jittery that I accidentally knock over the entire shelf. The safety glasses *and* the shelf crash to the ground with a series of thuds.

Parker's head snaps up.

"Sorry!" I call to the woodshop teacher, afraid she'll yell at me or kick me out.

Instead she laughs and says, "I see you take safety very seriously!"

I give her a weak smile and scramble to pick everything up.

To my relief, Parker hurries over and helps me right the shelf. Together, we put the safety glasses back in their place.

"Thanks," I say, my voice shaking.

"Are you okay?"

"Yup! Are *you* okay?"

"Uh-huh."

We stand there in agonizing silence for a second. Then we both start talking at the same time.

"I was prepping the foam—"

"Mr. Owusu said you were here—"

We stop and laugh nervously at each other. Then Parker says, "You go first."

I swallow. "I came to see if you needed any help."

"Sure. I'm almost done cutting the foam. I figured we should get a head start on that, you know?"

I nod and follow him to the table, relieved that he said "we." So he does still want us to work together.

Parker starts showing me which pieces he's already done and which ones still need to be measured and cut. I try to pay attention, but I can't help staring at his mouth the whole time.

"So what do you think?" he asks.

I blink, realizing I didn't actually hear the last thing he said. "Oh, um . . ."

He gives me an expectant look, and I know this is my chance to talk to him about what happened the other day and make sure we're okay.

But before I can force out the words, Parker sighs and says, "LB, listen. I don't want things to be weird with us, you know? I want us to be friends."

"Friends?" I repeat.

"Yeah. That's okay, right?"

Wait. Is he saying that's *all* he wants us to be?

Suddenly it dawns on me that I may have completely misread the situation. Maybe that day in his basement, he thought *I* was going to kiss *him*. That's why he ran off, not because of anything I said, but because he doesn't feel *that* way about me.

I fight back a wave of disappointment. Because of course I want to be friends with Parker. I love hanging out with him. And I definitely don't want things to be awkward between us anymore! And really, what did I expect? That he could forget about everything that happened this fall and like me back? (Okay, yes. Maybe I was hoping that could happen. But obviously that was just a fantasy.)

"Yes, friends is great," I say, forcing myself to smile. "Let's do that!"

He nods. "Okay, good. So . . . let's get back to work?"

"Absolutely," I say. But the disappointment lingers in my stomach like acid.

CHAPTER 19

A week later, I'm surprised to find Priya waiting for me at my locker after school. "Hey," she says. "Got a minute?"

"S-sure," I stammer. Talking to Priya alone always makes me feel like I'm in trouble with the principal or something. "Are we still on for another CFI meeting this week?" Now that Kat's not really speaking to me, I guess it doesn't matter if I go or not.

"Oh, yeah," Priya says. "But that's not why I'm here." She glances around as if to make sure no one is listening. "Owen said you gave him some advice a while back about . . . about our relationship?"

"Not exactly. I told him about some things I've been researching and he just ran with them."

"So you never told him to write me songs and take me on dates to stuffy restaurants and make me jewelry?" She holds out her wrist to show me the gaudiest bracelet I've ever seen, made out of beads that spell out "Owen + Priya 4-EVA."

"No!" I cry, trying not to laugh. "I would never, ever tell someone to make *that*!"

She sighs. "So why is he doing all of this? I thought we understood each other. That's why I decided to give this dating thing a shot. But the past couple weeks, Owen's been acting like a completely different person. And whoever that guy is, I do *not* want him to be my boyfriend."

Whoa. I knew the whole "Pumpkin" thing was weird, but I had no idea Owen had taken what I said and totally distorted it. "I think he's just nervous about messing things up."

"Well, all this stuff he's doing *is* messing things up!" Priya says. "And I don't know how to make him stop."

"Just talk to him." It's ironic, me giving someone dating advice. But she sounds so desperate. "No matter what, you two are friends, right? If you really trust each other and you're honest, then you'll be fine."

"I can try, I guess." Priya shakes her head. "I just hope that if things don't work out between us, they can go back to normal." Then she walks away.

As I watch her disappear into the crowd of kids, I think about that word, "normal." It's the whole reason I made up my Friendship Formula, so things between Kat and me could go back to how they used to be. But I'm starting to wonder if "normal" even exists.

That evening, Dad hands me a dusty photo album. "Look what Maisie found in the basement. So many cute pictures of you girls in here!"

I can't help smiling at one of my sister and me on a merry-go-round when we were both tiny. Maisie, of course, is holding on to my hand, making sure I'm okay. Protecting and guiding, as always.

"And check this one out," he says, flipping to a picture of Kat and me in our Hemlock uniforms. "That must have been, what, first grade?"

"Second." I can tell by my terrible bowl haircut.

That was the year Kat and I became inseparable. Until then, kids at Hemlock were still pretty nice to us. Then second grade hit and suddenly our entire grade was divided into kids Courtenay liked and kids she didn't. One day, Courtenay and her friends ganged up on me on the playground, and Kat came to my rescue. After that, I would have followed her anywhere.

Anywhere except back to Courtenay, I guess.

Suddenly my chest starts to ache. I close the photo album and place it back on the coffee table.

"Dinner's ready!" Maisie calls out.

We go into the kitchen to find another one of my sister's experimental dinners. It's some sort of stew, but it's hard to tell what kind.

"I might have cooked it a little too long," Maisie says as she ladles the greenish-brown glop into our bowls.

"Well, it smells good," Dad says, heading to his usual seat at the table.

He's right. It does. And yet, as we all settle in to eat, none of us can seem to bring ourselves to taste it.

Dad's phone buzzes, and he glances at it. "Oh, Mom's on her way home."

"Maybe we should ask her to pick up some Thai food?" Maisie says with a laugh. "Just in case this is totally inedible?"

"No," Dad says firmly. "You put a lot of work into this goo—I mean *stew*."

"And it really does smell goo," I add. "I mean *good*!"

We all look at one another. Then Maisie says, "So, on the count of three?"

"Let's do it," Dad says.

"One, two, three," I count off.

We put our spoons into our mouths in unison. There's a moment of silence as we chew and chew. And then . . .

"Wow," Dad says.

"Huh," Maisie adds.

"This is really good!" I chime in. The texture is a little crunchy and slimy at the same time, but the flavor is awesome. "Nice work, Mais! What's in this?"

She smiles, clearly relieved. "Let's see. There's carrots, chickpeas, okra, eggplant, tomatoes, and pineapple."

"Did you say *pineapple*?" I ask in disbelief.

Maisie giggles. "Yup! I thought it would give it something extra, you know?"

Dad shakes his head in wonder. "Wow, Mais. You certainly have interesting instincts when it comes to food," he says.

"I never thought I liked cooking, but it's actually super fun."

"Of course it's fun. It's like chemistry!" I say. Then I get an idea. "Hey, maybe we can sign up for a cooking class together? There's one starting at the Y in a few days."

Maisie's face lights up. "That would be great! But isn't that something you'd rather do with Kat? I remember you said you two have been trying out new things."

"Oh, um." I've been avoiding telling my family about my fight with Kat, since I knew seeing their reactions would just make me feel worse. But I guess I can't hide it any longer. "I'm not totally sure we're friends anymore."

Dad's spoon clatters into his bowl. "What? Since when?"

"Since last week?" But really, it's been a lot longer than that. I try to remember the last time things felt really solid between Kat and me. Even before I left Hemlock, there were times when we weren't on the same page. Back then we didn't have anyone else to hang out with, so it didn't matter.

"I'm sorry, kiddo," Dad says. "That's hard."

"You never know. You might patch things up," Maisie says. "Or you might reconnect when you're older."

I think of the way Courtenay and Ashleigh drifted apart for a few years and are besties again. Not that I want Courtenay as a friend, but I guess Maisie has a point. It's not impossible. Maybe this really is just some time apart like Kat said.

A moment later, Mom comes bustling through the door. "Oh, good, I didn't miss dinner," she says. Then she glances at what we're eating and her eyebrows shoot up. Clearly she's wondering if she should have taken her time getting home.

"You're just in time for stew," Dad says.

"Don't you mean *goo*?" Maisie says with a giggle.

"It's the goo stew special!" I cry.

The three of us start laughing again. Mom looks puzzled but she joins in too. And when we're sitting down and eating together, it turns out to be one of the best meals we've had in a while.

CHAPTER 20

When I get on the bus a couple of days later, I don't even bother looking for Kat or Parker. Instead I head right for my usual seat beside Ashleigh.

"Are you okay?" I ask. She looks a little green.

"Fine," she says, but it doesn't sound all that convincing. "Courtenay and I went to this indoor carnival last night and ate way too much cotton candy and then went on some rides and now . . ." She groans. "My body hates me."

"So the nostalgia trips are still going strong?" I ask.

"Yup! I think Courtenay's avoiding being home right now. Her parents are packing everything up before they put the house on the market."

Oh, I guess it makes sense they'd sell it if Courtenay's parents are splitting up.

"Any chance she's moving to another town?" I can't help asking.

"No, she wants to stay here with her mom," Ashleigh says. Then she laughs. "Lucky for me, that means our indoor water park trip is still on."

She doesn't sound very excited about the idea, but of course Ashleigh is too nice to tell Courtenay no. "You don't have to do everything she says, you know."

"I don't really have much of a choice," Ashleigh answers. Before I can ask what she means, she adds, "Any luck with Kat?"

I glance over my shoulder, but Kat's so far back, she can't hear us. "She still won't really talk to me."

"I'm sorry," Ashleigh says. Then her face lights up. "Hey, I think I have an idea that will cheer you up."

"What is it?"

"Come over to my house after school today and I'll show you."

"Ugh. I'm not really a fan of surprises." I definitely don't want a repeat of the Roller Derby disaster.

Ashleigh smiles. "Trust me. You'll like this one."

After school, I head home to drop off my stuff and then I jump on my bike and ride to Ashleigh's house a few streets over. The weather has been pretty mild lately considering it's the middle of winter, but today the icy wind is brutal. I'm glad it's a short ride.

When I get there, Ashleigh leads me up to her room. Just like her wardrobe, her bedroom looks like it's straight out of a catalog, with crisp cream-colored sheets and sky-blue curtains. It's also neater than my room has ever been.

"So, what did you want to show me?" I ask.

Ashleigh goes over to her carefully organized closet and pulls out a box. "My aunt got me this for Christmas."

I gasp when I see the picture on the side. "Oh my gosh, that's the exact crystal-growing kit I've wanted for ages!"

Ashleigh beams. "I figured you'd like it. Honestly,

I thought it was a silly present at the time, but now I'm excited for us to do it together."

"Can we open the box?" There's still packing tape on the sides.

"Sure. Can you get some scissors from my desk?"

I hurry over and grab a pair that's sitting next to Ashleigh's computer. I'm about to turn away when I notice a stack of colorful stationery on her desk. It reminds me of the letter I saw Courtenay reading at her locker. Maybe it wasn't a love letter but a note from Ashleigh wishing her a good day or something equally nice. But thinking about that letter makes me remember the "mean notes" Courtenay claimed someone was sending her. I've been so wrapped up in all the drama with Kat, I haven't really had time to puzzle out that little mystery.

"Found them?" Ashleigh asks.

"Yup!" I say, holding up the scissors. "Hey, has Courtenay said anything else about someone pulling pranks on her?"

Ashleigh frowns. "She mentioned something about gum on her bag. Oh, and there was that confetti thing.

But I guess either of those could have been an accident. Nothing since then, though. Why?"

I shrug. Courtenay accused me of being behind the pranks. But if she really thought that, then why hasn't she gotten me in trouble by now? Probably because she has no proof. But hey, if someone wants to mess with Courtenay, that's fine by me. I do wonder who else at Lincoln might feel the same way about her that I do.

"I was just curious." I hold up the box. "Ready?"

Ashleigh grins. "Let's grow some crystals!"

CHAPTER 21

When I get to set design the next day, Mr. Owusu sends me over to the stage to show Kat how my newly constructed fog machine will operate. I'm nervous about having to work with her, since we've barely spoken the past two weeks. But I have no choice.

"So this is what I came up with," I say.

The plan is for me to hide behind the back curtain right where Kat will be. I'll put the nozzle of the fog machine under the curtain, so when Kat is doused with water, the fog will waft out right where she's "melting." We'll put glow-in-the-dark tape on the stage so she'll be able to follow it off and behind the back curtain. When the fog clears, she'll be gone, as if by magic.

Kat listens, nodding but not really looking at me. When I'm done, she says, "Sounds good. Thanks."

And that's it. Our conversation is over.

She turns to leave, but I can't let her go yet. Not when I finally have a chance to say something.

"Kat . . ."

She stops. "What?"

I need to tell her I'm sorry. I need to tell her that I'll do whatever it takes to be her friend again. Time apart isn't making her miss me, apparently, and it's not making me any happier, either.

But the empty look she gives me stops the words in my throat. I used to be able to read Kat like an open book, but now she's a blank page.

"Um, you're going to make a great Wicked Witch."

It's supposed to be a compliment, but the way Kat rolls her eyes tells me it's the wrong thing to say. "Gee, thanks," she shoots back. Then she walks away.

Across the stage, Parker is having Courtenay practice walking through a cloud of bubbles. I watch as she giggles at everything he says and puts her hand on his arm for no reason. Ugh.

Okay, back to work. I turn to my machine and start adjusting the nozzle. I must pull too hard, though, because the entire thing comes off in my hand.

I don't realize how loud the cry of distress I make is until Parker rushes over to help me. "We need to glue it back on," I say, trying not to moan.

He nods and runs to grab a hot glue gun. He hands it to me and asks, "Do you want me to hold it steady while you put it back together?"

"Um, yeah. Thanks."

The whole time I'm reattaching the nozzle, I'm painfully aware of how close Parker is to me. His shoulder is only inches from mine. And yet it also feels like there's an entire galaxy between us.

When we're done fixing the fog machine, Parker sits back and says, "So I was thinking we should get together over February vacation to finish working on the tornado."

I swallow. The thought of enduring any more painfully awkward building sessions with him, of pretending I only have "just friends" feelings for him, is too much.

"You know what? How about I just finish the tornado on my own."

He frowns. "Are you sure?"

"Yeah, it'll be easier that way. You've already done a lot of work on it. I can take it from here."

"Well, if you're sure . . ."

I get to my feet. "Yup. It'll be fine. I got it."

Parker nods. "Okay. But if you change your mind, let me know."

"Thanks. You too," I say.

Gah! It's like we've gone back in time, and I'm as nervous around Parker as I was back when we first met. If I start yelling "Hydrogen!" at him, then we'll have officially regressed. I haven't blurted out any element names in a while, but I'm definitely under enough stress to go back to that particular calming exercise.

I guess this is exactly what Priya was afraid of with her and Owen. That if things didn't work out, it would make it hard for them to go back to being friends again.

But . . . but would I rather I'd never gotten to hang out with Parker, never had my stomach do little flips whenever he was nearby? No. As hard as it is to be around him now, I don't regret any of that. And things can't stay like this forever, right? I only wish they'd hurry up and get less weird between us.

That night, Maisie and I attend our first cooking class, which covers spaghetti, steamed vegetables, and sugar cookies. It's all pretty basic stuff, but we have a great time from the minute we start chopping tomatoes.

As we measure and mix and strain, Maisie laughs and says, "Wow, this is the first time I think I've actually followed a recipe."

I stare at her in horror. "If you improvised that much in science, you could blow up the entire lab."

"Good thing this is only food!" she says. "But maybe if I start following recipes, you'll actually eat what I make."

I laugh. "Hey, I had two bowls of that goo stew, remember?"

Maisie stirs the marinara sauce and glances over at me. "So what's all this about you and Kat not being friends anymore?"

"It's . . . complicated," I say, which feels like a serious understatement.

"Try me."

I sigh and consider what to tell her. And then, as our pasta water boils, I wind up telling her everything: about the Friendship Formula, about Courtenay, and about the science club.

When I'm done, Maisie nods slowly and asks, "Why do you want to be friends with Kat so badly anyway?"

I gape at her. "Are you kidding? She's my best friend."

"Okay, but why? You said yourself that you don't really have much in common."

"It's not just about having things in common. It's about . . . feeling like someone understands you, like they're on your side, you know?" Both things I didn't really think about when I was putting together my Friendship Formula, I realize.

"But it doesn't sound like you and Kat have really been on the same page lately," Maisie points out.

"That's because of Courtenay. Every time I make progress, she comes along and messes it up."

Maisie tips her head to one side, like she's not quite convinced. "It's funny," she says after a minute. "When I left Hemlock, I thought I'd stay in touch with all my friends. But now that I'm at St. Mary's and I'm focused more on school, things feel different."

"You still talk to some of your Hemlock friends, don't you?"

"Sure. But we've all got our own stuff going on now, and it's actually kind of nice. It gives us more to talk about when we get together. And I figure, the more friends the better, right?"

Of course my sister would take the rosiest view of the situation. But I guess she has a point. If I hadn't come to Lincoln, I wouldn't be friends with Ashleigh and Bree, or gotten to hang out with Parker. There's room in my life for people other than Kat. I only wish it felt like Kat still had room in her life for me.

CHAPTER 22

Over the weekend, I try not to think about Kat or Courtenay or Parker or any of the other drama at school. Instead I decide to "do science." But when I go through a few of the most recent Exploding Emma videos, the experiments all look so pointless. Yes, making things explode is fun. But I feel like my life has had more than enough explosions in it lately. I'd like to try putting something together rather than setting it on fire.

So when I see Mom stuffing envelopes for a big Valentine's Day fundraiser that she's planning, I offer to help. At least I can put my restless hands to good use.

"Thanks so much for your help, LB," Mom says. "These were supposed to go out last week, but things have been so busy!" She grabs another roll of stamps. "So, any big Valentine's Day plans this year?"

I groan. "Trying to get through the day?"

At Hemlock, Kat and I would give each other handmade valentines and then try not to get depressed while all the other girls showered one another—particularly Courtenay—with teddy bears and chocolates. The only good thing about Valentine's Day this year is that February break starts the day after, which means I'll have an entire blissful week off from school.

Mom laughs. "Come on, I bet it won't be so bad. You have lots of new friends now!"

"I wouldn't say lots, but I do have a few." I was already planning to make my usual punny card for Kat. She might not be speaking to me, but it's a tradition. Maybe I'll send one to Ashleigh and Bree too. (And to Parker? Since friends do that . . . right?)

"So Maisie's been raving about the cooking class you two are doing together," Mom says. "It's so nice to see you branching out and trying new things."

I start to roll my eyes. Usually when Mom says

things like that, what she really means is that she's glad I'm doing something other than the science-y stuff she claims not to understand. But then I think back to what Mom said, about how she's always been bad at branching out.

"Did *you* try new things when you were my age?" I ask.

"Not willingly," Mom says with a laugh. "I basically went along with whatever my friends were doing. It felt safer, you know? But now I regret not being braver."

I can certainly relate to that. The only thing I've ever felt comfortable doing on my own was science. But I guess I always had teachers (or Exploding Emma videos) guiding me through it, so I never felt alone.

"But you knew you wanted to do event planning, right?" I ask. "You did that on your own?"

Mom smiles. "Actually, no. My friend Lauren was planning a fundraiser for our college cheerleading team and she talked me into helping out. It turned out I loved it. But would I have tried it on my own without her pushing me? I don't think so."

I try to imagine what Mom would be like if she

worked somewhere else, but I can't. Her job is so perfect for her. She gets to socialize with people and help them at the same time.

"So you're saying I should keep challenging myself?" I ask.

"The way I see it, you already have," she says. "So keep up the good work!"

But I think about the way my Friendship Formula has messed things up between Kat and me, and between Priya and Owen, and maybe even between Parker and me. That doesn't feel like good work at all.

On Monday, I head back to Owen's house for another Carbon Footprint Initiative brainstorming session. We have one last chance to get the project in good shape before the final meeting with the principal.

But when I go upstairs, I find Owen and Priya are having some sort of face-off in the middle of the room while Bree worriedly looks on from Owen's desk.

"No, this plan is wrong," Priya is saying. "Principal Valenta will never go for it."

"I'm telling you, it'll be fine!" Owen cries.

Well. This is a far cry from how lovey-dovey they were at the last meeting.

"Um, hey," I say softly.

"LB, I'm so glad you're here," Bree says. "Maybe you can help us."

I swallow as Priya and Owen keep glaring at each other. I'm not sure I want to get involved in whatever this is.

"We're trying to come up with new ideas," Bree explains.

"But *someone* is too tied to what we already have," Owen says.

Priya lets out an exasperated sigh. "Trust me, the new ideas won't work."

"Trust you?" he says with a snort. "I'm supposed to trust the person who dumped me a week before Valentine's Day?"

"I didn't dump you! Things just felt so weird between us that I said we should take a break."

"Exactly. You *dumped* me," Owen says.

Whoa. I knew they were having problems, but I can't believe they actually broke up!

"Guys," Bree cuts in. "Can we just focus?"

But Priya shakes her head. "No way. If Owen won't listen to me, then I don't want to be here." She grabs her bag and storms out of the room. A minute later, we hear the front door slam.

There's a long silence. I glance at Owen. The blood seems to have drained out of his face.

"Maybe it's better if you go too," he says softly.

"What?" Bree cries. "But our meeting with the principal is right after vacation, and we have nothing!"

"Please," Owen says, his voice cracking. I've never seen him this upset.

Bree and I exchange a look. Then we get our things and quietly walk down the hall, leaving Owen alone in his room.

"I don't get what happened," Bree whispers to me.

But I do. This is all because of the bad advice I gave Owen and Priya. If it weren't for me, Owen would never have tried to "woo" her with cheesy songs and jewelry. And if I'd just kept my mouth shut, Priya wouldn't have tried talking to Owen about it and ruined their friendship—and the Carbon Footprint Initiative.

"Don't worry," I tell Bree. "I'm going to fix this." Somehow.

CHAPTER 23

During lunch, I've been mostly sitting alone at a table near the trash bins. Sometimes Bree will join me if Priya and Owen are being especially annoying. Ashleigh's offered to sit with me a couple of times, but I didn't want to make her choose between me and the rest of the group. Besides, being alone just feels easier.

So I'm surprised when Kat comes over at the start of lunch the next day and hands me a card.

"What's this?" I ask. An invite to her birthday dinner, maybe? It's coming up soon, and I haven't heard a word about it.

"An invitation to the art club open house on Thursday," she says.

Oh. But this is still good news. "You really want

me to come?" I hold the card gently in my hand, as if it might explode.

"Of course I do." Kat hesitates for a moment, as if she wants to say more. But finally she sighs and adds, "See you there?"

"Definitely," I tell her.

As she turns and walks back to what used to be our table, I carefully put the invitation in my bag. I can't help thinking this is a peace offering, that Kat is giving me one last chance.

A few minutes later, I'm finishing up my sandwich when a grape sails through the air and lands by my chair. I whirl around and see two boys grinning back at me. I don't recognize either of them, but I know the evil glimmer in their eyes. I saw it all the time when I was at Hemlock. To kids like them, a girl sitting by herself is a target.

The taller of the boys grabs another grape and chucks it at me. I duck out of the way, but it manages to graze my ear. I glance around, hoping a teacher saw it happen, but no one is paying attention.

I've been through this type of situation so many

times before that I know what to do. Keep my head down. Wait for it to be over. Don't make it any worse than it has to be.

Something flares inside me. *No.* I'm not going to be the scared mouse. I spent way too much time letting Queen Courtenay get away with this kind of stuff, and I won't do it anymore.

But before I can stand up to them, someone else stomps over to the boys. It's Courtenay.

Great. Is she going to join in? Give them some tips on how to be even better bullies?

To my surprise, she charges at the boy with the grapes and gets right in his face. "What do you think you're doing?" she snarls at him.

The boy snorts. "Nothing. We were just having some fun."

"Does it look like *she's* having fun?" Courtenay asks, pointing to me.

The boys look at each other. Then the taller one rolls his eyes. "Who even *are* you? Why is this any of your business?"

"Because I used to be a loser like you," Courtenay

says. Then she grabs the grapes out of the boy's hand, tosses them in the compost bin, and storms away.

I stare after her in shock. Did that really happen? Did Courtenay actually *defend* me?

My head swims as I try to come up with another explanation for what I saw, but I can't. Maybe I was wrong about Courtenay. Maybe she really is . . . evolving?

That night, I can't stop thinking about what happened at lunch with Courtenay and feeling like I should *do something*. But what?

I consider calling Ashleigh and talking to her about it—these days, I tell her almost everything—but I'm not sure what to say. Considering she and Courtenay hang out a lot, she probably knows anyway. Maybe Ashleigh was the one who encouraged Courtenay to make those bullies stop in the first place. But . . . somehow I doubt it. The way Courtenay shot them down, it really felt like it was coming directly from her.

I try watching a documentary on sea mammals, but my mind keeps wandering. I try listening to music and jumping around my room to get some of the jitters out of my body. Nothing works.

Finally I flop on my bed and do something I thought I would never do. I pick up the stack of graphic novels Kat lent me and start flipping through them. I start trying to read one and then another, but I'm having trouble understanding what's going on. I'm ready to give up, but then I remember how important this seemed to Kat. So I pick up one more, the one about the dragon, and start reading. And suddenly I'm hooked. I've never read anything like it and I would have never thought it was my kind of story, but it's amazing.

"You still up?" Mom asks, knocking on my door.

I look up and notice it's an hour past the time I usually go to bed. "Wow, I didn't realize it was so late."

"What are you reading?" She comes to sit next to me. "Is that a comic book?"

"A graphic novel."

Mom frowns. "What's the difference?"

"I . . . I have no idea," I say with a laugh, realizing I never bothered to learn. "I guess I'll have to find out."

CHAPTER 24

When I get to the art club open house on Thursday, I'm shaking with nerves. My plan is to go in, congratulate Kat, give her the flowers I brought her, and tell her how much I loved the graphic novels she lent me.

But getting Kat alone is tricky when there are so many people around. Luckily there's no sign of Courtenay yet. I still don't know how to feel about her after she stood up to those bullies the other day, but I don't want her around when I'm trying to finally patch things up with Kat.

As I wait for Kat to finish talking to Ms. Deen, I wander around the room, searching for her drawings. But I don't see any of her usual food superheroes. Maybe they're hanging up in the hallway. I do find a few paintings I really like. There's something about the way the primary colors play off each other that grabs my attention. Huh. Maybe I'm not completely clueless about art after all.

Even though I'm not in the art club anymore, I've actually been working on my Uncoordinated Girl comic in my spare time. It still looks pretty terrible, but I'm learning a lot about panels and motion lines and speech bubbles. And every drawing I do gets a little easier, which is encouraging.

Near the kiln, a charcoal drawing catches my eye. It's of two girls under an umbrella during a rainstorm, stomping in a puddle. I don't need to look at the name underneath to know the drawing is Kat's.

Suddenly I'm right back in that moment. Kat and I were in fourth grade. We were waiting for her mom to pick us up after school. It started to pour and instead of going back inside to wait it out, we huddled under the umbrella together and jumped from puddle to puddle. By the time Ms. Edwards arrived, we were soaked. She was furious that her fancy car was going to get wet, but we couldn't stop laughing.

I'd forgotten all about that day, but clearly Kat hasn't. I wonder what it means that she drew this. Is it her looking back at a time when we were simply friends, without any of the awkwardness and doubts that have started creeping in lately?

Next to it, I see another drawing. This one is of the same two girls, a little older now, and they're sitting in front of two different puddles, holding two different umbrellas. The space between them stretches on and on.

And then I see the third drawing. It's of two groups of people in two different puddles—but now the puddles look like planets. In one of the groups is a girl who's clearly supposed to be me, and in the other is a girl who's clearly supposed to be Kat. We couldn't look farther apart, with all those people standing between us.

Tears prick my eyes. Is this really what Kat thinks? That there's nothing connecting us anymore?

Suddenly, Kat appears next to me. "So what do you think?"

"They're . . . beautiful," I say. Because despite everything, they are.

"The series is called 'Evolution,'" Kat tells me.

I close my eyes for a moment. If this is how she sees us, is there even anything worth saving?

"Here, these are for you." I thrust the flowers into her hands.

"Thanks." She studies them for a moment. "Some of us were going to go out for ice cream after the open house if you want to come."

"That's okay," I say. "I . . . I have to get going."

"Are you sure?"

I nod. "Yeah, I—I told Maisie I'd help her make dinner."

"Lily—"

But I shake my head and only congratulate her again before I turn to leave. What's the point of sticking around? It's like her drawing. We're pretty much on two different planets now.

After I leave the art room, I spot a drawing in the hallway of a tree growing in the middle of a field. I recognize it right away as one of Kat's. I remember seeing it in her sketchbook. But when I glance at the name written underneath, it doesn't say Kat Edwards. It says Courtenay Lyons.

What? That doesn't make sense.

I turn to go back into the art room, to tell Kat what I discovered. But then I hear a familiar nasally giggle behind me.

Courtenay is at the end of the hall, holding hands with a guy. At first I think she and her ex-boyfriend have gotten back together. But then I see the guy's face and . . . it's not her ex. It's *Parker*!

My mouth drops open as I watch her lean over and whisper something in Parker's ear.

No. NO!

Suddenly it feels like a tornado has formed inside me. How could I ever think that Courtenay had changed? How could I be so stupid?

My body thrums with rage, desperate to lash out. I turn back to the drawing on the wall and tear it down.

"What are you doing?" Courtenay shrieks as she runs over to me. "That's mine!"

"It's not yours. You stole it from Kat! Just like you stole Parker from me! That's what you always do. You lie and steal and cheat. Maybe no one else can see how evil you are, but I can!"

Courtenay looks stunned for a moment. "N-no," she says. "I didn't . . . I'd never . . ."

"Of course you would!" I cry. "You did it all the time at Hemlock! You may have fooled everyone else, but I know what you're really like!"

I expect Courtenay to keep denying it, to hurl accusations back at me. Instead, tears start to trickle down her face. Then she turns and runs away, disappearing around the corner.

Nearby, Parker stares at me in shock. Wait. Did I really just say that about him being mine?

Before I can even try to explain, Parker shakes his head and goes after Courtenay.

And then Kat comes barreling out of the art room. "What is wrong with you?" she screams. But she's not yelling after Courtenay. She's yelling at *me*. "Why would you do that to Courtenay's drawing? Is this another one of your pranks?"

"*Her* drawing? What are you talking about? She stole it from you! I saw it in your sketchbook!"

"I had one like it that I told her she could trace for practice. But she added a whole bunch of stuff to make it hers. I told her she could use it for the show!"

I blink and blink again. "But . . . I was trying to help."

"By tearing down someone's work?" Kat cries. "What were you even thinking?"

I *wasn't* thinking. "I—I'm sorry. I'll fix it."

But Kat shakes her head. "Forget it, Lily. This isn't working."

"What do you mean?"

"Us! I thought if we had some time apart, things would be better. But . . . but I was wrong."

"No!" I cry. "That's not true! Things were finally getting better! My plan was working! Courtenay's the one who messed it all up!"

Kat freezes. "What plan?"

Oh no. But now that I've told her that much, I guess there's no point in hiding the rest. "A friendship formula," I admit. "A way to get you back, to get us to spend time together again."

"Is that why you suddenly got into art and comic books and Roller Derby—and *ketchup*? You were turning me into some kind of experiment?"

"No! I mean, maybe at first. But I really do like some of those things. Not ketchup, obviously, but the drawing part has actually been fun, and last night I even read one of the—"

"Enough," Kat says, and she sounds so disappointed. So betrayed. "I told you I don't want any more drama in my life, and the way I see it, ever since I came to Lincoln, all the drama has been coming from you."

I close my eyes, suddenly remembering the day of the science fair. It hits me that Kat's New Year's resolution had nothing to do with Courtenay. It was about me.

"I just didn't want to be on a different planet from you. Like in your drawing," I whisper.

Kat looks at me. "Lily, you really don't understand anything at all."

There's a long silence. I can feel tears pricking at my eyes, but I won't let myself cry.

"I told you," I say, trying to keep my voice from shaking, "my name's not Lily anymore. It's LB. Everyone else can learn it. Why can't you?"

Kat sighs and turns to leave. Then she pauses and says, "The umbrella was over all of us."

I blink. "What?"

"In the third drawing in my collection, the one with all the people. Yes, you and I were on different planets, but there was a big umbrella over all of us," she says. "At least, I thought there was." Then she shakes her head and walks away.

CHAPTER 25

I barely sleep that night. Instead I keep replaying the whole awful fight with Kat over and over in my mind. When my alarm goes off, I groan. It's Valentine's Day. I'm tempted to fake being sick and skip school, but I know my parents won't fall for it. So I drag myself out of bed, get dressed, and stuff my handmade cards into my bag, even though I'm not feeling particularly loving or lovable today.

On the bus, I keep my eyes down and go sit with Ashleigh. She's oddly quiet, and I'm afraid it's because she heard about what happened at the art show. Maybe she's regretting ever giving me a second chance.

I hesitate a moment and then grab a valentine out of my bag. "Here. I made this for you."

To my relief, Ashleigh's face lights up. "Wow, thanks, LB! I have something for you too." She pulls a little box of chocolates out of her bag with my name written on it in loopy cursive and hands it to me. Then she opens my card and giggles. "*Are you made of Copper and Tellurium? Because you're CuTe!*"

"I can never resist a chemistry pun," I say, popping a chocolate in my mouth. Then I lower my voice and ask, "You probably heard about what happened last night?"

Ashleigh's smile fades. "Parker told me."

The chocolate suddenly tastes bitter. Parker. He must hate me, not just for tearing down Courtenay's drawing but for saying that stuff about us.

"Is he . . . mad at me?" I ask.

"Not exactly. I think he's mostly confused."

I groan. "I'm such an idiot."

"No," Ashleigh says. "You thought Courtenay had stolen Kat's drawing and you were protecting her. If I were you, I'd jump to the same conclusion."

This is one of the things I've come to love about Ashleigh. She's always willing to take my side, even when I've messed up.

"Once Ms. Deen finds out what I did, I'll be in so much trouble," I say.

Ashleigh gives me a sympathetic smile. "Maybe if you explain what happened and apologize to Courtenay, it'll be okay."

But I shake my head. I don't want to apologize to Courtenay. She might not have copied Kat's drawing, but I can't get the image of her and Parker holding hands out of my head. She knew I had a crush on him and snatched him up for herself anyway. Ugh. I wish I could pour water on her and have her disappear in a cloud of smoke, just like the wicked witch she is.

"I know what will cheer you up," Ashleigh says. "Look how great our crystals look!" She grabs her phone out of her bag and shows me some pictures.

They really do look awesome. I can't wait to check them out next time I go over.

As Ashleigh is putting her phone away, I notice her fingernails are stained blue around the edges.

"Were you painting something?" I ask.

"Oh." She laughs. "No, I was making a cake last night and went a little overboard with the food coloring."

"What kind of cake? We're supposed to be baking a simple white cake in my cooking class next week."

"Yum!" Ashleigh says. Just then, the bus pulls up to the school and she jumps to her feet. "Hey, I have to go do something before first period, but I'll see you later?"

"Sure."

As I get off the bus, I spot Parker ahead of me, going up the school steps. If I could just talk to him, explain what happened, maybe he'd understand. I hate the thought of him and Courtenay together, but I hate the thought of him being mad at me even more. But when I call his name, he only ducks his head and hurries away.

My first Valentine's Day at Lincoln starts out better than I expected. Besides getting chocolates from Ashleigh, I also get a beaker-shaped cookie from Bree. She laughs hysterically at my card and promises to hang it up in her locker.

I debate about whether or not to give a card to Kat. She made it pretty clear that she didn't want to be friends anymore. But before lunch, I find an unsigned valentine in my locker that simply says "Happy Valentine's Day." It has to be from her. So I hurry over to her locker and slip one of my cards inside.

Then, before I can chicken out, I put one in Parker's locker too.

When I get called down to see the principal after lunch, I'm not even surprised. No doubt Courtenay told Ms. Deen what happened last night. I should be terrified of getting in trouble, but I'm actually oddly relieved.

"Lily Blake Cooper," the principal says when I go into his office. "Please have a seat."

I sink down in a chair, my hands shaking as I put them in my lap.

"Do you know why I've called you to this meeting?" he asks.

I nod, not daring myself to speak.

"We take destruction of property very seriously at this school," he says. "And while we don't have any eyewitnesses, I don't think you can blame me for suspecting you were involved."

I look up at him. No eyewitnesses? At least two kids saw me tear down Courtenay's drawing.

"I thought we put these pranks behind us, Miss Cooper," he goes on. "To say I'm disappointed is an understatement."

Okay, now I really have no idea what he's talking about. "What pranks?" I ask. He can't be talking about the confetti and stuff, can he?

He sighs. "Miss Lyons opened her locker today and found all of her belongings had been slimed."

My mouth sags open. Slimed? "Wait. You think *I* did that?"

"Are you saying you didn't?"

"Of course I didn't! Just because there's slime involved doesn't mean I'm to blame." Why won't anyone believe me when I say I'm done pranking people?

"All right. Then do you have any idea who might have done it?" he asks, leaning forward.

"No. But it definitely wasn't me!"

The principal sighs. Then he calls Courtenay into his office.

I expect her to strut in and start hurling accusations left and right. But she's surprisingly quiet as she sits in the chair next to me. Her shirt has a gooey blue stain on the front, no doubt from the slime.

"All right," Principal Valenta says. "Now that I have you both here, let's get to the bottom of this."

To my surprise, Courtenay shakes her head and says, "It's really not a big deal—"

"It *is* a big deal," he insists. "Plus, I heard there was also an incident at the art club open house last night. Is there a problem between you two that I should know about?"

I hold my breath, waiting for Courtenay to start dumping all the blame on me. But she only shakes her head and says, "No, we're okay. Right, LB?"

I study her face, sure this is part of some plan to mess with me. But there's no evil gleam in her eye. It really seems like she's serious.

"Um, right," I say.

Principal Valenta doesn't look happy, but since Courtenay doesn't seem to want to press the issue, he finally lets us go.

After we leave the principal's office, Courtenay

and I walk silently back to class. But the air around us feels full of things that need to be said.

Finally I can't stand it anymore. "Why didn't you turn me in?"

Courtenay shrugs. "I figure now we're even. You know, for the stuff I did at Hemlock."

I stop walking. Is she serious? Suddenly something inside me snaps and all the things I haven't been saying come pouring out.

"Do you even know how horrible life was for me there because of you? I came to school terrified every day. I had to *transfer* because of you! Do you really think a ruined drawing can even things out?"

Courtenay opens and closes her mouth like a surprised fish. I've never seen her at a loss for words before. "I was hoping . . ." she says finally. "I thought I could finally make things right." Then she straightens her stained shirt and slips into her classroom.

I keep walking toward math class, but it feels like my brain is trying to work out a complicated chemical equation. Just when I think I have Courtenay figured out, I'm thrown all over again.

Is she evil or is she nice? Has she changed or hasn't she? Does she think I'm behind the pranks or not?

Wait. The pranks. The blue slime on Courtenay's shirt. The blue stains on Ashleigh's fingers.

Suddenly the puzzle pieces click into place, and I realize how wrong I've been about everything.

CHAPTER 26

I look for Ashleigh on the bus ride home, but she's not there. I send her a message, and she writes back right away, saying she went home early. So after I get to my house, I hop on my bike and head straight to hers.

"Are you sick?" I ask when she opens the door. She looks fine, except for the lack of a smile on her face.

Ashleigh doesn't answer. Instead she waves me up to her room.

"I heard you got sent to the principal's office," she says, closing the door.

"It was you, wasn't it?"

Ashleigh's face pales. She doesn't ask me what I'm talking about. She doesn't even try to deny it. Instead she slumps down on her bed and nods.

"Why would you do that? Why would you prank Courtenay? I thought you two go way back."

To my surprise, Ashleigh lets out a bitter laugh. "Yeah, we do go way back. We've been forced together since we were in diapers. No matter how many horrible things she did to me, no matter how awful she was, my parents insisted that she didn't mean it, that she was just a kid, that I was overreacting."

"B-but you said you two were friends again!"

Ashleigh glances up at me and there are tears in her eyes. "I don't think Courtenay knows how to have friends. She only knows how to have servants."

I think of how Courtenay treated the Things back at Hemlock, yelling at them whenever they made the slightest mistake. But then I remember how she came to my rescue when I was being pelted with grapes and accused by the principal, and I don't know what to believe anymore.

"When our families drifted apart, I was so relieved. Finally I wouldn't have to see Courtenay anymore," Ashleigh goes on. "Then she showed up at Lincoln, acting like the helpless new girl, and my parents insisted I be nice to her, show her around. And suddenly we're best friends again."

"What did you write in the notes you sent her?" What I thought was a love letter must have been one of those mean notes. Courtenay just slipped it in her bag and acted like everything was fine, even though the words must have stung.

Ashleigh sighs. "'No one wants you here.' 'Go back to Hemlock.' That kind of stuff. I'm not proud of it. But I thought I could at least make her feel what I felt all those times when we were little, you know? Remind her that she can't pretend the past never happened."

"The confetti," I say. "Was that you too?"

She nods. "You know that movie *Carrie* where the girl gets sprayed with blood? When we were at camp one year, I had the lead in the play and Courtenay was jealous, so she rigged something up so I'd get doused with tomato sauce during the final scene."

My mouth sags open, although I don't know why I'm surprised. It's exactly the kind of thing the Courtenay I knew back at Hemlock would do. "And of course she got away with it," I say.

Ashleigh rolls her eyes. "She convinced some younger girl to help her and that girl wound up getting blamed for the whole thing. I tried to tell the counselors what really happened, but it was my word against Courtenay's."

Figures. The exact same thing happened to me at the sixth grade dance. It was my word against Courtenay's, and why would anyone listen to me over the queen of the school?

"I'm so sorry, Ashleigh," I say. "I can't believe your parents would make you hang out with her after everything."

"You know she used to make fun of me for not having a mom?" Ashleigh says. "But my dads don't seem to remember that. All they care about is that Courtenay's 'going through a tough time right now.' And yes, I know her parents are splitting up and her family is struggling. But just because she's having a hard time doesn't suddenly make her a nice person!"

I can't help smiling. "I was starting to think I was the only one who didn't think she could change."

"So, you'll help me?" Ashleigh says, her eyes wide and hopeful.

"Help you? With what?"

"Pranking Courtenay might get her out of our lives. I figure if she feels the way we have, she'll be so miserable at Lincoln, she'll have to transfer, right?"

"But where would she go? Her family's staying in town and she can't afford to go back to Hemlock."

"No, it's only her mom who's staying in town," Ashleigh says. "Her dad's moving to a different state. If she goes with him to start over somewhere else, we would be rid of her for good."

My head spins. Courtenay living in a completely different state sounds amazing. It would be like a dream come true. No more worrying about what she's really after. No more watching her with Parker. And no more of her turning Kat against me.

Kat.

I picture her disappointed face if she finds out I really am pulling pranks again. And after everything that happened this fall, do I really want to go down that path again?

"No," I say. "I can't." I'm not that person anymore. I don't *want* to be that person anymore.

"This is Courtenay we're talking about. After everything she's put you through, don't you want her out of your life for good?" Ashleigh asks.

"But she *is* gone. The old Courtenay is anyway." As I say it, I realize it's true. That awful girl at Hemlock who lashed out at people and blamed them for her own mistakes doesn't exist anymore. The new Courtenay might still be a work in progress, but then again, so am I.

"So we're just supposed to forget everything she did?" Ashleigh says. "She didn't even apologize!"

"Not exactly. But she tried." In fact, when I think back, I realize that Courtenay has been trying to make amends ever since she came to Lincoln and I didn't want to see it. "I think she's been trying with you too. That's what all those nostalgia trips are about. It's her way of making things right."

"Well, things aren't right. I don't know if they'll ever be right!"

I nod because I understand. "I might never completely forgive her, either," I admit. "But I'm tired of hating her. It brings out the worst in me. And, I mean, look at you, Ashleigh! You're the nicest, most forgiving person I know. You're not someone who plays pranks and gets revenge."

Ashleigh lets out a sob. "I don't want to be! But having Courtenay around again, I think it's changed me."

"It feels like it's changed me too," I say. And not for the better. "But that doesn't mean we can't *keep* changing, right? We can do it together?"

Ashleigh nods, tears trickling down her face. "I'm so glad we're friends now," she says.

As I go to hug her, it hits me that we're not just friends. Somewhere along the way we became *best* friends, even while I was still clinging to Kat. I was so desperate to keep things from changing that I couldn't see that they already had.

"If I help you make peace with Courtenay, can you help me with something too?" I ask.

Ashleigh nods and wipes her eyes. "What do you need?"

"I have to throw the best birthday party ever."

CHAPTER 27

February vacation goes by in a blur of planning. Ashleigh and I spend hours figuring out the details for Kat's surprise party. We decide to have it the day before her actual birthday so she won't be expecting it. And it will be the same day as opening night of the play, which will either make everything more exciting—or a whole lot worse.

In between party-planning sessions, I work on building the tornado for the play. The whole project is taking a lot longer than I expected, and I could kick myself for insisting to Parker that I could do it on my own. But I'm determined to get it done in time.

I message with Bree a few times, trying to think up some ideas for the Carbon Footprint Initiative, but nothing we come up with seems like it will meet Priya and Owen's high standards. *We need to get them talking to each other again*, Bree finally says. But that's easier said than done.

The nice part is that Mom took the whole week off from work, so we get to hang out a bunch. We sample some of Maisie's inventive recipes, which I must admit are getting better and better. Mom and I even don some rubber gloves and help Dad and Maisie finish cleaning out the Spider Basement.

It all feels like the calm before the storm. I don't hear from Kat the whole time, and I'm so busy all week that I barely have time to wonder what she's doing.

But there is someone I do keep thinking about over school vacation: Courtenay.

Finally, by the end of the week, I can't stand it anymore. I need to go see her. So I convince Ashleigh to ride her bike over to Courtenay's house with me.

Her house, of course, is giant. Mine could probably fit in the garage. But there's also a big "For Sale" sign out on the lawn and a stack of boxes in the driveway, so I can't really be jealous.

"Are you sure about this?" Ashleigh asks. "What if she doesn't want to talk to me?"

"It'll be fine," I say. "Just wait out here for a few minutes and I'll let you know when it's time."

Ashleigh chews on her lip, clearly worried. But she nods and goes to sit on the sidewalk, out of sight behind some bushes.

I go up and ring the doorbell. Courtenay opens it dressed in stained sweatpants, her hair in a messy ponytail. I've never seen her look so disheveled. "LB," she says. "What are you doing here?"

"Um, can we talk?"

"Sure. I was just packing up my closet, but I can take a break."

She leads me inside, and I'm surprised by how bare the house is. Even though I've never been here before, the emptiness feels wrong. There are only a handful of rugs scattered throughout the downstairs and a few random chairs, but the rest of the furniture is gone. Our footsteps echo off the bare walls.

"Looks like you're almost moved out," I comment.

Courtenay nods. "My dad moved into his new place

a few days ago. And my mom's dropping a bunch of stuff off at our apartment. She should be back soon."

She plops down in the middle of a rug, and it's so strange to see her sitting there. Like the queen of a kingdom that's slowly crumbled around her. I hesitate for a moment and join her.

"So," she says.

"So." I reach into my pocket, pull out a small bottle, and hand it to her. "Here."

Courtenay frowns. "You're giving me slime?"

"Apology slime. It's sort of my thing. When I really mess up, I give it to someone and tell them they can dump it on my head if they want to."

"How many times have you messed up that badly?" Courtenay asks with a laugh.

I can't help smiling. "Too many. But I'm serious. Take it."

Courtenay takes the slime and cups it in her hand. "Thanks. But really, you should probably be the one sliming me."

"Um, I think someone already beat me to it."

Courtenay blows out a slow breath. "It was

Ashleigh, wasn't it? I was talking to my therapist about it, and I realized that you weren't the only one at Lincoln who had reason to hate me."

"I think she was just really angry."

Courtenay leans back and peers up at the vaulted ceiling. "You know what's funny? My Hemlock friends couldn't dump me fast enough after they found out about my dad being a thief. Brent broke up with me at a Christmas party in front of everyone. It turned out they all hated me. And the sad thing is, I knew it all along and I didn't care." She shakes her head. "When I saw Ashleigh again, I thought I could finally have a real friend, you know? Like you and Kat."

Something stabs at my heart. Is there even a "me and Kat" anymore?

"But all the stuff you did to Ashleigh," I say. "The tomato sauce, the things you said about her family—"

"I was jealous. My parents were fighting all the time, and Ashleigh had this perfect family. It felt like, no matter what I did, she was always better." Courtenay looks at me. "It's why I was so awful to you too."

I blink. Is she saying she tortured me at Hemlock

all those years because she envied me? "What could I possibly have that you were jealous of?" I ask in disbelief.

"Are you kidding? You were one of the smartest kids in our grade." She rubs her eyes, and I notice how tired she looks. It's a far cry from the picture-perfect queen bee she was at Hemlock. "I'm sorry I was horrible to you. I tried to apologize after I got to Lincoln, but . . . saying 'I'm sorry' is not something I have a lot of practice doing."

"You're a work in progress. We all are." I get to my feet. "Ashleigh's outside. She wants to talk."

"Really? I sort of figured she'd never forgive me."

"She might not," I admit. "But she's willing to try." I head for the door, but Courtenay stops me.

"Parker and I are just friends, you know," she says. "He was only holding my hand at the art show because I was so nervous about people seeing my drawing."

"Oh."

"When he and I were working on the bubble machine, he spent half the time talking about you. How amazing you are and how great your special effects project was going." She gives me a little smile. "I thought you should know."

I don't even know what to think about that, so I just say, "Thanks."

I go outside and wave Ashleigh over. "Courtenay's ready to talk," I say. Then I hop on my bike and ride away, not daring to let myself hope that what Courtenay said about Parker is true.

CHAPTER 28

When I get back to school on Monday, the first thing I see when I go inside is Priya and Owen arguing in the lobby. Their final meeting with the principal is in four days. At this rate, the whole Carbon Footprint Initiative is going to fall apart before it's even started.

I'm about to keep walking, but then an idea hits me.

"Hey," I say, going over to them. "Can I give you some advice?"

They both glare at me. I don't blame them for not wanting to listen to anything I have to say after what happened last time.

"This isn't about relationships, I promise," I go on. "It's about science, which I know a lot more about."

"What is it?" Priya asks.

"What if you had the science club members come up with ideas for the CFI, and have *them* vote for winners? I mean, you two aren't the only ones in the club. Shouldn't other people have a say?"

"But . . . it's my project," Priya says.

"And we're the president and vice president," Owen adds.

"What about everyone else? They've put in a bunch of work helping you two, and you never even asked them if they had any ideas."

They look at each other. "That's true," Owen says. "I guess . . . we're used to running the show ourselves."

"It's always been just the two of us," Priya adds.

"Okay, but maybe that's not working anymore. Maybe you need more people on your planet."

They look confused, but I don't know what else to say. So I only shrug and add, "Think about it, okay?" It's the best I can do.

The dress rehearsal for the play Friday afternoon is a disaster. Part of the backdrop falls over, the sound cues come in at the wrong times, and my fog machine won't even turn on. Mr. Owusu assures us that hiccups are normal before opening night, but I'm so nervous that I feel like I might throw up.

As Mr. Owusu gives notes to the actors after the run-through, I hurry backstage to work on the fog machine. No matter what I do, it just won't turn on.

Ugh. What was I thinking building a special effects machine? I have no idea what I'm doing!

I'm considering just tossing the whole thing in the trash when Parker comes over. "Need some help?" he asks.

It's the first time he's even looked at me since the art club open house. I was starting to think he might hate me. But then I think about what Courtenay told me. Maybe it's possible he doesn't hate me after all.

"Yeah, sure. Thanks," I say.

We get to work, taking the machine apart and checking all the parts to make sure they're working properly.

"Thanks, by the way," Parker says after a minute.

"For what?"

"The valentine. It was funny."

"Oh. You're welcome. You know me and science puns."

He nods. "I'm sorry mine was so boring."

"Yours?" I ask.

"Yeah. You got it, right?" The look on his face is almost hopeful.

Then it hits me. The plain card that simply said "Happy Valentine's Day." I thought it was from Kat. Wait, Parker gave me a valentine?

Is it possible . . . ? Does that mean . . . ?

Right then, the fog machine sputters to life. We both jump in surprise and then laugh.

Mr. Owusu hurries over, excited at the sight of the fog filling up the stage. "Great work, you two! You make an excellent team."

Parker smiles at me. "Yeah, I think we do."

That night, Bree calls me, her voice shaking with excitement.

"LB, your plan worked! Priya and Owen got everyone in the science club to submit ideas for the CFI, and then we voted for our favorites."

I blink with surprise. Wow. Priya and Owen actually listened to me?

"What did the principal think?" I ask.

"He loved them! He said we can implement at least half of them by the end of this year."

"What? That's amazing!"

"I know! Thank you so much for your help," she says. "I was starting to think we'd have to scrap the whole thing."

"How are Priya and Owen doing? Are they still, you know . . . ?"

Bree sighs into the phone. "I'm not sure. They're fighting a lot less, so that's something. I don't get it. They're so alike. Doesn't that mean they're perfect for each other?"

"Maybe." But having a lot in common doesn't necessarily mean you're compatible with someone. My Friendship Formula might have been a bust, but it did show me that.

CHAPTER 29

Saturday afternoon, Ashleigh and I hurry over to the roller-skating rink to set up for the party. We have an hour to get everything ready before Taylor brings Kat for what she thinks is another Roller Derby practice.

Jayla arrives a little while later with a few of her friends from the play in tow. *Kat's friends*, I correct myself. They bring easels that Jayla borrowed from Ms. Deen and set them up around the party room.

"Who's leading paint night?" Ashleigh asks me.

"Or paint *afternoon*," Jayla corrects her. We have to be done by dinnertime so we can all eat and head over to school to get ready for opening night of the play.

Before I can answer, the door opens and Courtenay comes in holding a case full of art supplies.

Ashleigh's eyes widen. "You asked *Courtenay*?"

"She's actually a pretty good artist," I point out.

"I know, but . . . are you okay with having her here?"

The funny thing is, I *do* want Courtenay here. I'm not sure the two of us will ever really hang out, but it would have felt wrong not to invite her.

"She is friends with Kat now," I say. "I'm not saying everything is forgotten. But we're trying to evolve, remember?"

Ashleigh nods and takes a deep breath. "Right. Okay, let's go get her set up."

When we head over to Courtenay, she gives us a nervous smile. "Thanks for inviting me. Where should I put my stuff?"

"What do you think, Ash?" I ask.

Ashleigh glances around the room. "How about near the window?" She waves Courtenay forward, and I watch as they walk off together. They both look stiff and uncomfortable, like strangers. I guess in a way they are. Their talk the other day was a good first step, but if they're ever going to be real friends, they'll have to get to know each other all over again. Maybe it'll work and maybe it won't. I guess that's the thing about friendships—you never really know where they'll end up.

Just then, Maisie arrives with the cake. She's frosted and decorated it to within an inch of its life. It's glittery and neon and blinding—and perfect.

"Wow, this looks amazing!" I say. "Is that chocolate?"

Maisie giggles. "Yes, but . . ." She lowers her voice. "Don't tell anyone. I added zucchini. It tastes awesome."

"Well, if it tastes as good as it looks, then I don't care what's in it." I glance toward the door and am shocked to see Priya and Owen. Huh. Bree must have invited them. Last I checked, they didn't even like Kat. But the more the merrier, I guess.

"Need any help setting up?" Owen asks.

I can't help staring as I realize that he and Priya are holding hands. "Um, no, we're good. Thanks."

Priya must see that I'm staring, because she says, "You should probably know that Owen and I are taking a temporary leave from the science club."

I blink. "What?"

"We're stepping down from our positions," Priya says.

"You were right. The club is full of people with platinum ideas," Owen says. "It's time we gave them a shot."

"And it'll give us time to work on our relationship." Priya gives Owen a little smile. "See if we can finally figure out how to do this whole more-than-friends thing."

"That's great!" I say. "You two really are so perfect together."

Priya shrugs. "As long as Owen never calls me 'Pumpkin' or sings to me again."

"Hey!" he cries. "You try rhyming a word with 'proton.' It's not easy."

To my surprise, Priya actually laughs. "Yeah, okay. Maybe I'll give you another shot." Then they head off to get something to drink.

I can't help smiling as I watch them bantering back and forth. Maybe they really will figure things out. And if they can laugh about the ups and downs of their relationship, it gives me hope that they can stay friends, even if things don't last.

An alarm goes off on my phone. Uh-oh. It's almost time for Kat to arrive. I ask Maisie to go outside to warn us when she's here while I start handing out party hats.

I'm putting on my own hat when I spot Parker coming toward me.

"Sorry I'm late . . . as usual," he says with a smile.

I'm so relieved to see him and to hear him actually talking to me that I can't help grinning back at him and saying, "Thank you." Then I blink and add, "Um, I mean, thank you for coming."

"Listen, I—"

But whatever Parker was going to say is interrupted by Maisie calling, "She's here! Everyone hide!"

We all scurry behind tables and chairs while Maisie flips off the lights. Then we wait. Beside me, I can hear Parker breathing. I don't know how I can tell it's him, but I can.

"Practice is in here today," I hear Taylor say as she leads Kat into the back room.

Then the lights come on and we all scream, "Surprise!"

Kat looks more shocked than I've ever seen anyone look. "Wh-what is this?"

"Happy birthday!" I say. And then everyone else chimes in with a chorus of happy birthdays.

Kat goes from looking shocked to looking overwhelmed. "Thank you," she starts to say, but she can't even get the words out because she's crying.

I hurry over to her with a tissue.

"You did this for me?" she asks.

"You said you wanted a party this year. So I figured a manga/paint night/Roller Derby shindig should do the trick. A mix of old and new, right?"

She nods. "It's perfect!"

"I'm sorry, Kat. I know I gave you a hard time about not trusting me, but I should have trusted *you*. I was so scared we'd stop being friends that I came up with that stupid formula and I should have just—"

"It's okay," she breaks in. "I think we were both getting used to things being different. I want us to be friends. I miss you. But I need my own life too, okay? I think we both do."

"I know. I want that too."

She nods and wipes her eyes. Then she glances over my shoulder. "Whoa, are we going to be painting dragons?"

"Yup! Actually, I got the idea from one of the graphic novels you gave me."

"Oh yeah? Which one?" It's obvious she doesn't believe me.

"The one about the dragon prince turning into a human. Those illustrations were amazing. Like that scene at the end where he's falling through the clouds and his wings are shriveling up? So cool!"

Kat laughs in surprise. "I know. Wasn't that amazing? I can show you how to do that cloud technique. It's actually pretty easy."

"Nice!" Who knew the two of us could ever talk about art together? "Maybe we can do another art lesson sometime."

"Sure, LB. That sounds fun."

A warm bubble of happiness expands in my chest

at the sound of her finally using my new name. "Oh, I almost forgot!" I hold out a gift bag. "Happy birthday."

She opens it—a T-shirt with a picture of a spotted cow-like creature on it—and squeals. "An Oriflax shirt! How did you know I've been dying for one of these?"

"Duh. Because we're friends," I say. "And there's one more thing in the bag."

Kat peeks in and takes out a piece of paper. "A ticket to the anime exhibit tomorrow? But I already have one of these."

"I know. This one's mine. I figured you could give my ticket to Hector."

"But . . . but it's our tradition. You really don't mind if I go without you?"

"No," I say, and it's true. "Hector is super into anime. You two will have a great time." Really, I should have thought of it sooner.

It's like in Kat's drawing. We're still under the same umbrella—but that umbrella has gotten a lot bigger. It doesn't need to be only the two of us anymore. That's why my Friendship Formula was all wrong. It didn't take into account the fact that relationships aren't just between two people. There are other molecules bouncing around all the time, affecting them. Maybe the way people stay friends no matter what is by knowing when to stick together and when to bounce apart.

"We can hang out next weekend, okay?" she asks.

"Sure. So, are you ready to party?"

Kat smiles. "Totally!"

And we do.

CHAPTER 30

The play that night is amazing. Jayla is adorable as Dorothy, Hector is hilarious as the Cowardly Lion, and Kat has a ball playing the Wicked Witch. But it's Courtenay who steals the show. She looks so confident up there, so in charge, with a halo of bubbles floating all around her. I never thought I could buy her as a good witch, but somehow it's exactly right.

Parker's bubble machine works perfectly, and it adds so much to the show. I should never have doubted him—or Courtenay.

There is a slight hiccup with the tornado. It starts spinning the wrong way and nearly sends Jayla flying off the stage. But we manage to get her off safely, and I doubt anyone else even notices.

After the first two special effects are off our plates, Parker and I crouch behind the back curtain in the dark, waiting for our cue to fire up the fog. I can hear him breathing beside me, his face only inches from mine, and it sends tingles down my spine.

Suddenly, in the darkness, it feels like I can say anything to him, like I can finally be brave on my own.

"Hey," I whisper.

"Hey," he whispers back.

"You remember that day at your house when we almost . . . kissed?"

"Yeah?"

I'm so relieved that was what was happening, I almost laugh. Instead I take a breath and whisper, "When I said I was sorry, it wasn't because I didn't want to kiss you."

"Oh."

"I was apologizing for all the silly things I did last fall. I guess I couldn't believe you'd want to kiss me after everything that happened."

"That was a long time ago," he says.

"Yeah." It certainly feels that way now.

"So," he says after a moment, "you're saying that you *did* want to kiss me?"

I swallow. "Yes."

"Oh." I swear I can hear him smiling. "Okay. That's good to know."

Onstage, Kat is just about to get doused with water. That's our cue!

FLICK!

Fog starts billowing out onto the stage, and it's a thing of beauty. Kat milks her big "I'm melting" death scene and then vanishes into the fog. The audience erupts into applause, and I know we nailed it.

When it's done and the machine flicks off, Parker and I both start laughing silently. Then he takes my hand and squeezes it, and I smile and squeeze back.

After the show, everyone is hugging and high-fiving. I can't remember the last time I felt so swept up in the excitement of a group. Science club is nothing compared to this. I'm already thinking about next year's show. Who knows, maybe I'll even start a special effects club.

"LB!" someone says, rushing over to me. It's

Courtenay, and she looks so . . . happy. "That was amazing!"

"You were incredible," I tell her. And I mean it.

"Thanks." She leans in and whispers, "You and Parker are so cute together. I'm happy for you." I realize that for the first time, I actually believe her.

I head back over to Parker, and he takes my hand in his. As we walk around together, it feels like some sort of dream.

When Kat sees us, her eyebrows shoot up. Then she flashes me an "I knew it!" grin.

I let go of Parker's hand and hurry over to hug her. "Your death scene was incredible!"

"Thanks to your fog machine. I really felt like I was melting!"

"I guess we make a pretty good team," I say.

Kat smiles and gives me one more squeeze. "Yeah, I guess we do, LB."

"Hey, I was thinking. What if I started going by Libby?" It feels like after everything, I might need a new name for the person I'm becoming. If people can evolve, why not names?

"That's cute!" Kat says. "Whatever you go with, I promise I'll remember this time." Mrs. Clark starts calling everyone over for a cast photo. "Oops, gotta go. But you're going to the party after, right?"

"Yeah. I'm getting a ride over with Parker and Ashleigh."

"Cool. So I'll see you there?"

"Totally," I say.

Kat hurries over to her new friends while I head back over to mine. And even though we're on opposite sides of the room, it feels like we're finally where we're supposed to be.

ACKNOWLEDGMENTS

Every book takes a village. Thank you to Amanda Maciel and Talia Seidenfeld for helping me continue Lily Blake's story, and a huge thanks to the whole Scholastic team. As always, thank you to my agent, Ammi-Joan Paquette; to my critique group and writing partners; and to my family, especially Ray and Lia. And, of course, endless thanks to my readers.

Popularity? She's got a formula for that!

Lily loves science and hanging out with her best friend, Katie. But after a *really embarrassing* incident, she jumps at the chance to switch schools. She's ready to start over. With the scientific process, anything is possible!

After a summer spent coming up with theories and prepping for the switch, Lily starts her new school as Blake, a popular girl with a cool name, ready to climb the social ladder.

But every hypothesis has its flaws, and Blake will have to adjust her experiment as she adjusts to her new classmates. And when Katie suddenly shows up in Blake's world, things get messy. Who's got the winning formula: Blake or Lily?

Read the latest **wish** books!